THE BAD F

JOHN BLACKBURN was born in 1923 in th the second son of a clergyman. Blackbu near London beginning in 1937, but his education was interrupted by the onset of World War II; the shadow of the war, and that of Nazi Germany, would later play a role in many of his works. He served as a radio officer during the war in the Mercantile Marine from 1942 to 1945, and resumed his education afterwards at Durham University, earning his bachelor's degree in 1949. Blackburn taught for several years after that, first in London and then in Berlin, and married Joan Mary Clift in 1950. Returning to London in 1952, he took over the management of Red Lion Books.

It was there that Blackburn began writing, and the immediate success in 1958 of his first novel, *A Scent of New-Mown Hay*, led him to take up a career as a writer full time. He and his wife also maintained an antiquarian bookstore, a secondary career that would inform some of Blackburn's work, including the bibliomystery *Blue Octavo* (1963). *A Scent of New-Mown Hay* typified the approach that would come to characterize Blackburn's twenty-eight novels, which defied easy categorization in their unique and compelling mixture of the genres of science fiction, horror, mystery, and thriller. Many of Blackburn's best novels came in the late 1960s and early 1970s, with a string of successes that included the classics *A Ring of Roses* (1965), *Children of the Night* (1966), *Nothing but the Night* (1968; adapted for a 1973 film starring Christopher Lee and Peter Cushing), *Devil Daddy* (1972) and *Our Lady of Pain* (1974). Somewhat unusually for a popular horror writer, Blackburn's novels were not only successful with the reading public but also won widespread critical acclaim: the *Times Literary Supplement* declared him 'today's master of horror' and compared him with the Grimm Brothers, while the *Penguin Encyclopedia of Horror and the Supernatural* regarded him as 'certainly the best British novelist in his field' and the *St James Guide to Crime & Mystery Writers* called him 'one of England's best practicing novelists in the tradition of the thriller novel'.

By the time Blackburn published his final novel in 1985, much of his work was already out of print, an inexplicable neglect that continued until Valancourt began republishing his novels in 2013. John Blackburn died in 1993.

By John Blackburn

A Scent of New-Mown Hay (1958)*
A Sour Apple Tree (1958)
Broken Boy (1959)*
Dead Man Running (1960)
The Gaunt Woman (1962)
Blue Octavo (1963)*
Colonel Bogus (1964)
The Winds of Midnight (1964)
A Ring of Roses (1965)*
Children of the Night (1966)*
The Flame and the Wind (1967)*
Nothing but the Night (1968)*
The Young Man from Lima (1968)
Bury Him Darkly (1969)*
Blow the House Down (1970)
The Household Traitors (1971)*
Devil Daddy (1972)*
For Fear of Little Men (1972)
Deep Among the Dead Men (1973)
Our Lady of Pain (1974)*
Mister Brown's Bodies (1975)
The Face of the Lion (1976)*
The Cyclops Goblet (1977)*
Dead Man's Handle (1978)
The Sins of the Father (1979)
A Beastly Business (1982)*
The Book of the Dead (1984)
The Bad Penny (1985)*

* Available or forthcoming from Valancourt Books

THE BAD PENNY

JOHN BLACKBURN

VALANCOURT BOOKS

The Bad Penny by John Blackburn
First published London: Robert Hale, 1985
Reprinted from the large print edition published Bath: Chivers, 1986
First Valancourt Books edition 2014

Copyright © 1985 by John Blackburn

ISBN 978-1-939140-86-9 (*trade paperback*)
Also available as an electronic book

Published by Valancourt Books, Richmond, Virginia
Publisher & Editor: James D. Jenkins
20th Century Series Editor: Simon Stern, University of Toronto
http://www.valancourtbooks.com

All rights reserved. The use of any part of this publication reproduced, transmitted in any form or by any means, electronic, mechanical, photocopying, recording, or otherwise, or stored in a retrieval system, without prior written consent of the publisher, constitutes an infringement of the copyright law.

All Valancourt Books publications are printed on acid free paper that meets all ANSI standards for archival quality paper.

Set in Dante MT 11/13.9

PREFACE

Zzikki – hizzikki – aghizzikki? Ford wasn't sure what the words meant, but he knew their implications – will-power, concentration and prayer. Also chastity; the means to make contact without physical transmission.

'Yes,' Ford said, though the room appeared empty and he was quite alone. 'Yes, I've got that. The man's name is Tanek – Igor Tanek, and his train leaves at 7.45. That is quite clear, but how will I recognize him, please?

'Age about sixty-three, five foot seven inches tall and heavily built.' (Though nobody spoke, Ford noted the answers on the back of an envelope.) 'Dark hair growing thin on the top, a grey suit and a grey tie, and probably carrying a brown leather brief case.

'And he may have the case open and be looking at its contents.' Ford frowned at his notes and then laid them aside. 'But that description might fit a hundred other passengers, sir. Any middle-aged businessman flicking through a briefcase. Surely you can be more specific?

'Ah, a gold tooth, eh. That's much more helpful.' Ford smiled as he jotted down the information. 'Never liked men with gold teeth. My father had one.' Ford thought about his father and the smile widened. No, he hadn't cared for Dad at all. Dear old Dad with his flashing smile and his flashy ways. Daddy boy was in hell now, which was where he deserved to be. He had mocked the Church and deserted Mummy. Hell was the place for him. Ford hoped he'd remain there for many years to come. Let the bastard fry on the road paved with his own bad intentions.

'But I'm sorry, sir. Very sorry, Mr Aghizzikki.' The voice in his head had spoken again and Ford hadn't taken in its message. 'I don't understand you. I am a man of peace – a good Christian, so why do you ask me to do such a thing? I do not know the man called Tanek. Never spoken to him, so why – why – why must I commit such a terrible crime?'

'Because I desire it, Mr Ford. That is enough, so stand up and look out of the window.' The imagined voice became louder and louder. It shook the room and rustled the curtains. The words had to be obeyed and Ford crossed the room and drew back the curtains. Through the glass he saw a bus draw up and pick up passengers on its way to the station. Almost the last bus, though not quite. There would be more; many more. Across the street a clock struck six-thirty and there was over an hour left.

'I know that you are a man of peace, Ford,' the voice said. 'But I am a man of authority, and have given you an order. Obey my orders, Ford. Go to the station, take the train to London. Find Mr Tanek on that train, and then kill, or try to kill him.'

* * *

Why did the man in the opposite seat keep staring at him? He had work to do. He was trying to finish a manuscript. Mr Igor Tanek tried to concentrate on his papers and ignore the eyes of his companion. Little pink eyes with little pink flecks in them. Eyes which didn't appear to focus quite correctly unless they were turned in his direction.

'*Chapter Ten – The Head of a Traitor,*' he wrote, as he had planned to write, because he was paid to write – very well paid.

'Thomas Ryde was born in London, 1923 – the second of three children.' Balls, he thought as the carriage lurched and his pen slipped on the page. Everyone knew where Ryde was born, so concentrate on what you have learned yourself and ignore the man facing him. That short, tiny figure couldn't do him any harm, so think about Ryde and all you know about him. Hell's bells, they've paid you enough for the story. A thousand pounds for travel, another thousand for extras, and half the profits of the book when – if it was ever published.

If ever? Balls again, because Messrs Tupper and Brown had assured him that the book would appear if he did his researches satisfactorily.

'Our client is a wealthy man, Mr Tanek, and we can give you a free hand in every way,' John Brown had said, fingering the collar of his jacket and smiling like a grotesque china Buddha. 'In any reasonable way, that is. Take your time, but don't waste it either. The book should appear in our next autumn's list, so we need the synopsis by May.'

Well, Mr Brown and his client should have their material by tomorrow, if only that damn fellow would stop staring at him. Though why should he be worried? A sad, haunted stare from the eyes of a ghost, but what was wrong with that? He was a ghost himself – a ghost writer.

Yes, that was the correct term, as his agent had told him. 'You have no real originality, Igor, and little creative talent, but something almost as important. An ability to listen to another person's story and write it down. In this instance, the story of Thomas Ryde as dictated by our client.'

Well, he'd listened and he'd done his best, though there wasn't much to write home about. Tanek frowned at his notes. The client had sent him to Europe and he'd gone. For almost a month he had travelled about Germany, interviewing witnesses, and the facts were clear, the history books correct. Ryde was dead. He had died or been killed during an Allied bombing attack towards the end of the war and there was no story. The client's approach was haywire. Wrong premise, wrong deduction – wrong treatment.

Everything was completely wrong and the eyes of his fellow traveller still bothered him, though he didn't know why. The man was a pipsqueak, a puny dwarf, a seven-stone weakling as Charles Atlas, the famous muscle-builder, had described the type years ago. The pipsqueak couldn't harm him, so why should he be worried? The train was almost empty and he could move into another carriage. Why were those pink-flecked eyes disturbing? Tom Thumb, the seven-stone weakling, had joined the train at Dover, but so had another hundred perfectly respectable human beings.

Almost at Canterbury now. They'd be in Victoria soon, so forget the probing eyes, have a cigarette, relax and take things easy. Tanek reached in his pocket and took out a packet. He reached again and found that he had no matches. He felt despair and frustration and then forced himself to smile at his companion.

'Can you give me a light, sir?' he said. 'I'm afraid I'm out of matches.'

'Of course, sir,' Tom Thumb replied, reaching in his own pocket. 'Most happy to oblige,' he said and something came out. Something that looked far too heavy for his tiny hand.

CHAPTER ONE

9 p.m. – Victoria Station. The lights dim in the vast, echoing hall, and fog drifting up from the Thames to join the odours of grease, sweat and grime.

I leaned against the pillar to the right of the first arrival platform and I might have been waiting for a girl, if I had one, but I hadn't got a girl. I hadn't any mistress, thank God. I'd shuffled off Peggy Tey months ago, and all Bill Easter had was a master. A harsh, male taskmaster who enjoyed delivering threats and issuing orders.

'I wonder if you would mind doing me a slight favour, Bill?' the boss had said, but he didn't mean it. The old bastard knew that I minded. All I wanted to do was to strangle him, shoot him, slay him alive, though how could I? The blackmailing brute could read me like a book and he'd made a book of my career. A slim volume lodged in his bank with a note stating that it was to be sent to the Public Prosecutor if he came to an untimely end.

Murder – assassination – theft – extortion! The ancient swine had me by the short hairs and he'd listed my crimes under chapter headings. 'The Death of President Asmonda' was one. 'The Affair of the Cyclops Goblet' another. 'The Story of a Callous Murder' was number three, and he could sell me down the river like a southern slavehand. That was why I was waiting at Victoria to meet an overdue boat train.

'The 7.45 p.m. from Dover is still being delayed by works on the line and is expected to arrive at 9.30.' The Tannoy boomed overhead, and I looked at my watch and then at the huge soot-encrusted clock overhead. Twenty minutes gave me plenty of time for a drink and I headed for the nearest bar, stepping carefully around a pile of rucksacks by the door.

'Extraordinary this business about Halifax, sir.'

'I beg your pardon.' I'd ordered a large Scotch and turned

politely to a little buster with an evening paper beside the bar. 'What's been happening at Halifax?'

'Not the town, but the murderer, sir. John Halifax, the York hatchet man. Found him this morning working as a lavatory attendant, at Slough of all places.' He turned a page towards me and sipped at his half-pint glass. 'Makes you think, doesn't it? Two years and six months ago, this chap cut up his invalid mother with an axe. Left her body in the house and then makes off. Gets hold of another man's insurance card somehow and changes his name to Smith. For almost three years he goes scot free, and must have thought he was in the clear by now. Then, quite by chance, a rozzer spots him in a public convenience at Slough. You know, once those boys get their hooks into you, you've had it.'

'I'm sure you're right,' I said and gulped back half of my whisky. 'Two and a half years is a very long time.' Though I didn't know the unfortunate Halifax Smith, I felt rather sorry for him. Doubtless the invalid matriarch was a tartar who had fully deserved the hatchet. I'd like to deliver a few blows towards another invalid – my crippled patriarch of a master.

Still, two to three years was not really a very long time. Not when compared to almost forty. I turned away from my bar companion and thought about what the general had told me. A man who had done the worst thing in the world and then vanished. He and the other man. The man who, after such a long time, had claimed to know something. Who had been given the general's telephone number and arranged this meeting.

A meeting, which in spite of my resentment I was rather looking forward to. The second man would be almost home by now. Lurching home in a railway carriage with the information which could close a file. I didn't know what the information was, but if possible I would turn it to my own advantage.

'The Dover boat train is now approaching platform 3.' The loudspeaker drowned my thoughts and I finished my drink, nodded affably to my newspaper-reading pal and strolled out into the hall.

As was to be expected from the time of the year, the train was almost empty and I stood by the barrier and watched the handful of passengers trickle past. A few students, a group of children, one or two weary businessmen and a fat chap who looked slightly tight. But no sign of the man I had been ordered to meet. No stocky figure clutching a brown briefcase came striding towards me, and I became impatient. Mr X must have missed the damn train or caught another. He could have changed his mind and taken an aircraft to Heathrow from Berlin, Paris, Timbuctoo or wherever his journey had started. He could have done many things, but they were no affair of Mr Easter's – no business of mine. I'd carried out my part of the bargain. Massa had made a cock-up as usual, and the serf could call it a day and head for home. Or could he? A large Negro driving a trail of trolley trucks towards the barrier made me change my mind. Massa might be very angry if Rastus didn't make sure. Massa's contact could have had a heart attack or fallen asleep. The contact could have done anything and I'd better be sure. Anything, certainly the price of a platform ticket, was better than a life sentence in prison.

Better thirty years of Europe than a cycle of Cathay. I'd been drinking before I got to the bloody station and I remember that I hummed a line from 'Locksley Hall' as I purchased the ticket and handed it to a chap with a face like an outraged turkey cock's. I remember clambering up into the first carriage and finding nothing. Nothing in the second or the third or the fourth, but at last, in the sixth, I found him.

Mr X lolled back on his seat and he looked as though he was asleep, though the sight of him made me damn near vomit. His eyes and his mouths were wide open, and I deliberately use plurals for both organs. Two mouths, and one was in the normal position, the other was lodged between the jaw and his Adam's apple.

To use a cliché, his throat had been cut from ear to ear. To be honest, I was too sickened to notice whether he had bled a great deal.

CHAPTER TWO

'Well, Bill. You've seen the end of the story, so let's have a look at the beginning.' I'd reported back to the jail house, and Massa was not pleased. His horrible voice rasped as he read my notes, his horrible eyes scowled at the report, his horrible hand twitched as he finished the last page.

'Tanek,' he said. 'Igor Tanek – occupation: hospital orderly. Hobby – ghost writing and editing books by other persons. Obsession – hounding former Nazi war criminals. Nothing very wrong in any of that. All that friend Tanek did wrong was to get himself killed whilst delivering the material – my material, Billy boy. Priceless stuff which has taken me half a lifetime to compile.' Massa, whose real name was General Charles Kirk, a former chief of British Army Intelligence, left his desk and crossed to an enormous electric fire, which was turned on full, though the day was warm and the room stifling. 'No, nothing very wrong about Tanek's career, but his death annoys me considerably, Billy Boy.' He paused and massaged his fingers before the fire: all seven fingers. Three had been shot off his right hand, years ago and it resembled a talon, mottled with grey scar tissues.

'Four months back I was introduced to Tanek by a publisher who was interested in my memoirs, naturally.' The general straightened smartly and reached for his cigar case. 'He swore they were first-rate stuff and might turn out to be a best-seller, if a professional was persuaded to knock 'em into shape. By professional he meant friend Tanek, of course, and I hired him. Promised the feller £2,000 and fifty per cent of the gross profits, Bill, and gave him my only copy of the script. How could anyone be so foolish, my boy?' He paused to light his cigar. And how indeed, I thought. During the war, the British Intelligence Corps had not been noted for extreme efficiency, and Kirk's gullibility proved the point. 'Tanek was by birth a Polish Jew, taken to Auschwitz when he was ten years old, and maybe that's why I hired him.

'He knew Ryde, you see. He'd looked on the face of the Devil in 1944 and he shared my suspicions. Pocketed a thousand pounds, took a fortnight's leave of absence from the hospital where he worked and set off for Europe.' The general had lit his cigar and puffed a cloud of smoke into my face. 'Not sure where he went, but this morning he telephoned me to say he was coming home and the case was as good as completed. Gave me the times of his train, and that's why I sent you to meet him. A pity he was dead on arrival, but one can hardly blame you for that.' I should damn well think not, was the obvious reply. Somebody had slashed pal Tanek's throat a good half-hour before I found him and the blood had started to dry. Tanek was a back number and I hadn't killed him. But some person or persons had, and I wanted to know more about the individuals responsible.

'Tell me, General,' I said. 'Let's forget about Tanek for a moment and talk about Ryde – Tommy Ryde. What was he really like?'

'It's a long time ago, Bill,' he replied, and shuffled over to a filing cabinet. 'Almost forty years ago and I was only with him for about half an hour, when he came to me for his security check. You've read the details about that, and I can't say anything more, but I think – yes, I think that I liked him.'

Kirk unlocked a drawer of the cabinet and pulled out a heavy buff folder. 'Yes, I trusted Tommy Ryde, and not because of his background. Father – a highly respected clergyman of the Church of England who'd been badly wounded during World War One. Mother, a Frenchwoman, and Tom spoke her language like a native. Only a boy of twenty at the time, but I felt he could have been one of the best agents we ever had, though that's not why I trusted him. He had a strange quality, and his face and voice were surprisingly attractive.' Kirk's own voice and his heavy, well-bred features were completely without expression. 'It wasn't like being with another human being, but a machine that had been tuned to win one's personal approval. Uncanny, hypnotic maybe, but so flattering and appealing. Tom Ryde was quite certainly a bad penny. Maybe the worst human being I've ever encountered, but at the time I liked him.' He paused and handed me the book. 'Take a look at him, son. It's all there, as far as we know. A private hobby of mine. A scrap album devoted to the devil.'

I opened the folder and saw that it contained a mass of pictures; beside each picture there was a date and a note in Kirk's sprawling hand. The first photograph had been crudely tinted in colour, and it showed a child standing before a Georgian house. The child was wearing a sailor suit with very wide bell-bottom trousers and 'HMS *Royal Oak*' printed on his cap band. His eyes were very pale blue and he held a Dutch doll in his hands. The doll had no eyes; they had been removed. I turned the pages and the child started to grow older. The sailor suits changed to Eton collars and football jerseys. The school groups changed to young men and women in punts and on bicycles. Almost everything changed and only one thing remained constant. The boy's expression did not alter. An expression of cunning, false hope and a plea. The face of the Buddha – the eyes of a race-course tipster. I opened the last page and the story stopped. The punts and the bicycles were taken away, the Oxford bags faded, and the girls in their summer dresses had gone home. In the final photograph only the boy remained and he was quite alone; staring towards the camera in a black uniform with familiar armbands.

'I see what you mean.' I closed the book and laid it aside. 'And did anyone suspect Ryde's leanings before he went over?'

'Not as far as I know, Bill. And did Tommy Ryde have any pro-Nazi leanings? I believe his defection may have been caused by mere perversity and the wish to hurt.' Kirk blew another cloud of smoke towards me, and reached for something else in his drawer. 'Ryde and two other men were dropped over northern France in May 1944, and though his companions vanished or were killed by the Germans, he made contact with the French Maquis and transmitted us a number of messages which were later found to be false. The Resistance group were rounded up and shot by the SS a few months afterwards, but Tom Ryde was not shot. After the Normandy invasion, he came into the open and – listen to him, Bill.' Kirk pressed a switch on the thing he had taken from his drawer and I heard a voice.

'This is Thomas Ryde, a former British agent, talking to you from Hamburg. Before giving you the recent news, I would like to deliver a personal message of condolence to Mrs Mary Preston of 19, Cavenham Road, London SW14.' As Kirk had said, Ryde's voice was appealing, almost hypnotic, and my flesh crawled. 'Mary, my dear, I am very sorry to tell you this, but your husband, Private Ronald Preston, was captured outside Lille, this morning.' A slight pause and Ryde did sound really loving, compassionate and full of pity. 'To save Ronald's life, it was found necessary to amputate one arm and both his legs.'

'Yes, Bill, and I honestly liked the bastard.' Kirk had switched off his recorder. 'His tone sounds warm, sympathetic and loving on the radio, doesn't it? Gives a feeling that he's genuinely concerned and sorry about your predicament, and would like to help.

'Bastard! Bloody, treacherous, sadistic bastard.' The general's maimed right hand thumped the top of the cabinet. 'But it wasn't just the broadcasts. There were other things – things that happened in the camps.

'You know about evil, Billy, me son, though not the real extent of evil. Take a man's purse or his life and you're in trouble – serious trouble. But the theft of the soul is so much worse. To use every force, physical, moral and sexual for just that end, is the worst thing of all, and Ryde used them.' The old fool's crippled claw still hammered the cabinet to register annoyance. 'Lieutenant Brown-rigg yielded to drugs. Able Seaman Spence to torture. A bevy of harlots converted Captain Parr, and Ryde supplied the harlots.' The senile face flushed in righteous indignation. 'Just three examples, but all traitors – all made by Tommy Ryde, and there must have been at least a hundred others.

'Do you know what my dream of victory was, Billy Boy?' I shook my head and he answered the question himself. 'Hoisting a Union Jack over my house – getting tight in Piccadilly Circus, or singing "Rule Britannia" and "The Star-Spangled Banner"?

'No, nothing like that, Bill. Just a simple, unimportant thing. The punishment of that bad, vile man.'

'I understand, General,' I said, to show that I approved of his dream, though it appeared pretty meaningless. 'But a bit late in the day now, and didn't the Germans do the job much earlier?'

'Maybe – possibly – perhaps.' He mouthed the words and frowned. 'Ryde made his last broadcast from Hamburg on 20 December 1944, but he visited Stalag 32, a prisoner of war camp, three weeks later, and then vanished completely.

'As you know, I was with Montgomery's army when the war ended, and I tried to look for him, but what did I find? Not a trace. It was as if Ryde had been swallowed up or buried alive. All the notes, every file on him, had been destroyed on the orders of Himmler himself, and one of his colleagues at the radio station had been forced to commit suicide for merely mentioning the feller's name.

'I can't remember how many SS officers I interviewed afterwards, but a great many, and I got the impression that even to the worst of 'em, Tommy Ryde was somehow obscene – something too evil to talk about.' Kirk sat down and the chair creaked beneath his bulk. 'Well, after a while, I became convinced that Ryde was dead; probably liquidated. I closed the official files and I kept just that.' He grinned at the folder in front of me. 'Then, when I retired, I wrote my memoirs and hired friend Tanek to verify the facts and jazz 'em up a little, which he did.

'Ah, excuse me, Bill.' His telephone was ringing and he reached out and answered it. 'Charles Kirk speaking.' He sounded quite indifferent for a moment, then tensed. 'Ah, it's you, Superintendent. What? Please hang on a moment.' His hand scrabbled for paper and pencil. 'Go on now. There was a visiting card in his wallet to prove identity. The body was found five miles north of Canterbury, and you found the knife with his prints on it. The wallet too, but no sign of any papers.

'What!' His hand travelled rapidly across the page as he listened. 'You're sure of that, Super; quite sure? I see, and you'll be in touch again when you have more details. Thank you for ringing, Superintendent Blaker. Thank you very much indeed.' He banged down the receiver and stared at me with a look of complete bewilderment in his eyes.

'After you rang me from Victoria, Bill, I naturally got in touch with a pal at Scotland Yard, and that was my pal now.' Though his cigar was only half finished, he stubbed it out in an ashtray. 'A nut killed Tanek. A ruddy nut cut his throat and stole my manuscript. Chap called Ford. Definitely unbalanced, been in and out of mental homes for years. The train was crawling when Tanek died, so his killer climbs out, taking the briefcase with him and waits for the carriages to pass. Waits quite a long time, opens the briefcase and scatters my documents to the winds.

'It was blowing hard this evening, and God only knows where they are now or why Ford killed himself for good measure. Put his head on the rail for the next train to sever the neck, which it did. Any ideas, Bill?'

'Only that the murderer was a psychopath, General Kirk.' I crossed to a window and watched the dawn creeping over London. 'An irrational individual, no logical motivation for his actions. Case closed in my opinion.'

'Yes, I thought you'd say that, Bill Easter, but you're wrong.' Kirk snorted his contempt. 'Either you're deaf or frightened or you haven't been listening to what I said about Ryde. Tommy Ryde used psychopaths in his own filthy business. Tainted men's minds and rotted them.' He stood up and moved to the filing cabinet again. 'The case isn't closed – not on your Nellie. It's wide open and you're going to make a study of mental health.

'Careful about that part, however. Be a bit different from your normal line of country and a damn sight more dangerous. Not that that worries me in the slightest, but I don't like people who commit murder and then kill 'emselves for good measure afterwards. Don't like 'em at all.' He had found what he wanted and held out a stack of indexed cards. 'Here's a list of all Ryde's known contacts in England before he set out for France in '44, and you're going to make a start by visiting the survivors.

'Can't be many of 'em now – mostly dead. *Anno Domini, felo de se*, disease, accidents, and war of course. Always war, but there's one battle we haven't fought – not yet.' He grabbed his folder and opened it at the picture of the boy with the eyeless doll.

'Hello, son,' he said, and he wasn't speaking to me but to the face beneath the sailor's cap. 'We thought you were dead, didn't we? "Cold in the earth and the deep snow piled above thee, Tom." Well, we may have been right, but if we're not, if you're still alive and anywhere on this planet, I'll make you a promise.'

He closed the book and winked in my direction. 'Bill Easter has killed at least four people, and he's going to get you, Tommy Ryde.'

CHAPTER THREE

The snack bar or canteen could have been anywhere. The same plastic trays, the same racks of crockery, the smell of food and coffee, the same customers sitting at the tables or queuing at the counter.

I followed my host between the tables and glanced with interest at the clientele, though on the surface there was nothing remarkable about them. Every age group and every physical type were displayed. Over a hundred men enjoying light refreshments, and what was odd about that? Nothing at all, as long as you didn't look too long at the faces and see what was hidden behind them. The eyes – eyes of rejection.

'This way, Mr Easter.' Dr Marton led me through the restaurant and nodded affably at some of the customers as he passed them. 'Through here, please. Not far now.' Marton was a short, hearty man who shouted as he went, and his feet thudded the floor like pistons. 'Yes, here we are – my sanctum.' We had walked down a long, white corridor and he flung open a door on the left. 'Take a pew, if you can find one, and please excuse the mess. Never manage to get things straight nowadays, and probably never will. I said sanctum, but maybe den or cage might be more appropriate terms.' He hurled a pile of papers from a chair beside the desk and grinned as I sat down. We were in a large, untidy room which smelled strongly of leather bindings, pipe smoke and antiseptic, and book cases covered three of the walls.

'Well, Mr Easter, I've seen your letter from General Kirk, and though I don't know him personally, I know about him. Read his articles in the newspapers, watched him on television, and he's obviously been a pretty big pot in his time. So how can I help?'

'Tanek, eh. Tanek and Jimmy Ford.' He considered the question for a moment and reached for his pipe. I considered my own position and the line of approach. Old Kirk might have been a big pot once, about thirty years ago, but he was wrong, and Tom Ryde was dead. As dead as a doornail and I had no intention of wasting time on the defunct traitor, who'd shuffled off his mortal coils long ago. Why waste time on him or his contacts, when a recent crime was far more interesting?

Interesting and more profitable. If I could solve the story before the police, I might get a fair sum for my information to the press.

'Yes, the police have already spoken to me about that unfortunate business, Mr Easter,' Marton replied and my hopes dwindled. 'Not much to say about it really, but I'm at your service. Let's have a drink and discuss matters.' He opened a cupboard labelled 'Confidential Reports – Strictly Private,' and produced a bottle and a couple of glasses.

'Scotch OK for you? Good, my only real tipple.' I had nodded and he filled both glasses to the brim, but didn't add any soda or water. 'What exactly do you hope to find out, Mr Easter?

'I see. A motive and a link between the two men.' He handed me a glass and filled his pipe while I explained the situation. 'Nothing very sinister about the unfortunate Tanek, as far as I know, though one knows so little about the brain and its malfunctions. Came to this country following the Hitler war, after a pretty bad time, and was employed by the Health Service before retirement.

'Cheers.' He took a swig of Scotch and smiled widely. 'Tanek worked in over half a dozen mental care centres like this since 1946 and I couldn't fault him, but Ford – Jimmy Ford was a different subject. I didn't actually deal with him myself, so let's try to have a word with the specialist who did.' He moved another stack of papers and lifted a house phone. 'Helen,' he said. 'Could you spare me a few minutes, please? I have somebody here who wishes to discuss one of your patients.'

Apparently his contact had time to spare, and Marton replaced the receiver and grinned. 'Tell me, Mr Easter,' he said. 'The police know that Tanek was attacked by Ford on the train from Dover and probably died of his injuries. They know that Ford committed suicide soon afterwards. But where do you and General Kirk fit in?'

'Sorry, Doctor, but I am not at liberty to answer that.' I prepared to adopt the kind of Official Secrets Act manner which one of Kirk's official minions might have used, but mercifully it wasn't needed. There was a sudden rap on the door and a brisk, middle-aged woman marched into the room.

'God, what a slum your office is, Tony,' were the first words she said after Marton had made the introductions and found her a seat.

'Well, Mr Easter, I'm pretty busy, so shoot.'

'Right.' I'd shot and Dr Helen Grace, for that was the female's name, considered the enquiry. 'A connection between Tanek and Jimmy Ford? Well, there must have been, seeing that one got killed by the other.' Dr Grace had a clipped, no-nonsense voice which made me think of a governess shepherding groups of children across a park and seeing they didn't get out of line. 'You'll probably not understand what I'm saying, Mr Easter, so I'll try and explain as simply as possible.' She frowned at Marton's pipe and glass of whisky.

'Ford came here suffering from acute depression, and one can't blame him for that. Only child and the mother, who was a widow, had what amounted to religious mania – of the Anglo-Catholic variety. Saints and sacraments – everything, except the Pope, in fact.

'And if you must smoke that thing, Tony, don't blow it in my direction, please.' She raised a hand and waved it at the grey cloud ostentatiously.

'There was a long history of mental illness in the family, Mr Easter, and Jimmy Ford had been in other institutions for years. Some symptoms of hereditary syphilis too, though I don't believe that had much bearing on his case.

'Jimmy was admitted here as a voluntary patient, six months ago. Voluntary indeed.' She repeated the word with contempt. 'Depression, my foot. He broke into a church at two o'clock in the morning and was found weeping at the altar. Although the little bastard only weighed nine stone and stood less than five foot four in his socks, it took the combined strength of three rozzers to get him into the van.

'Well, I tried all the usual treatments for depression on him.

Even used insulin, but it didn't even scratch the surface, made no contact at all, and I decided that I'd got a bad schizo to deal with.

'No, schizophrenia is not normally dangerous, Mr Easter.' I'd merely clicked my tongue, but she turned on me like a blight. 'But when the condition is coupled with paranoia, you get trouble – dead trouble.

'Tell me, young man, have you ever been in a country which has suffered military defeat?'

'Several, Doctor. Vietnam, for one. Leonia was another.' I was preparing to list the countries involved, but the abominable woman soon cut me short.

'Then you may be able to understand what I'm talking about. One of my dearest friends comes from Prague and she was in the city before the war, when the Nazis marched in. She said that under the surface people tried to play a kind of game. To pretend that everything was as before. Every broken institution existed. Pure fantasy, of course. On the practical level there was hunger, chaos and often terrible violence, but between the layers there was something else. The people were waiting for the old institutions to creep back and take over.

'I believe that applied to Jimmy Ford's brain, Mr Easter, though Dr Marton does not believe in my theory, and he's the boss.'

She looked coldly at the poor old boss, who had let his pipe go out and had finished his whisky. 'He says that I'm being unscientific and keep rambling on about the supernatural. Well, so I am, Mr Easter, and why not? Witches have always been great healers, and mania and diabolical possession are often interlinked.'

'Why?' For somebody who had just sneered at the Anglo-Catholic Church, that seemed a bit far flung, so I popped her a question. 'What vacuum in Jimmy Ford's brain did he wish to fill, Dr Grace?'

'His mother, of course, Mr Easter. Mummy died soon after her boy was entered here, and he wanted her back.' There wasn't a single crack in Grace's self-confidence. 'Cancer killed Mrs Ford, but Jimmy refused to believe that. He met Tanek here and knew he was responsible.

'Tanek was a Jew, and the Jews rejected Christ, so the race became tainted. Tanek killed Mummy, and revenge is said to be not only sweet but a method of restoring life. I could offer you a hundred instances of this, Mr Easter, but, unfortunately, time is short.' She glanced at her wrist watch. 'I have other patients to see, so please excuse me.' She stood up, bowed and marched away like an officer on parade. Five minutes later, I left too.

⋆   ⋆   ⋆

It was dark when I left the hospital, and raining. Raining hard with the drops pounding on the concrete, like a forest of steel spikes planted upright. I groped my way to the car, climbed in and switched on the ignition.

Nothing – nothing at all. Two faint glimmers of light on the dashboard, a faint wheeze from the starter, and then silence, apart from the rain drumming on the roof. The battery was flat, my good old faithful banger had let me down, and I cursed Messrs Tucker and Hicks, the louts who'd last serviced her. I also cursed the manufacturers, who had neglected to fit a starting handle. 'Quite unnecessary, these days – modern alternators never give trouble – why strain yourself cranking the motor, when present-day electrical systems are virtually faultless. I presume you are a member of the AA, sir, and they'll soon get you out of any trouble.'

Balls! A cheap confidence trick, to keep the garages in business, and I wasn't a member of the AA. The damned vehicle was backed against a wall, and the parking space sloped upwards. If two hefty men gave me a shove, the engine might fire, but I could see no men about to do the shoving. And even if the motor did start, I was a hundred miles from London and the damn bitch might conk out on the way.

Old Marton could give me a bed for the night, I thought, and then changed my mind. He could, but the bed might be in a mental ward and no thank you. Bill Easter needed somewhere to sleep, but he's choosy about his sleeping companions, and another alternative came to sight. Across the road stood a tall, gaunt building with a sign reading: 'Mactaggart's Select Restaurant and Guest House.'

I climbed out and ran through the storm, for the shelter of Mr Mactaggart.

A wise move, as I thought then, though there was no Mr Mactaggart. He had died a long time ago and the property had been bought by a person who introduced himself as Smith. Mr Smith was surprised that I had no luggage, and was saddened to say the restaurant was always closed on Wednesday nights. But he did have a room to let, and sympathized with my predicament if – providing – of course, I could show that I was a respectable guest, naturally, and I did so at once, paying cash in advance out of the money Kirk had given me for travelling and sundry expenses. Mr Smith counted the notes and became affable. Though the restaurant was closed, the girl could cut me up some beef sandwiches, and if I could do with a drink, she could provide that too.

I could do with a drink, Scotch if it was available, because I was soaked to the skin. Smith ushered me into a cold, cheerless sitting-room on the first floor and reluctantly turned on a single-bar electric fire, before leaving. I waited for my repast and considered what I had learned at the hospital, though it was precious little.

Anti-semitism, my foot. Tanek might have been Jewish, but that hadn't killed him. Ford, being a religious maniac, might not have liked the Jews because they rejected Christ, but that didn't make him a murderer. Tanek had died for quite a different reason, and Dr Helen Grace had added two and two together and discovered that the total came to six. I'd come a long way for nothing, my clothes were wet through and my car was kaput. I was sitting in a chilly, damp room, massaging my hands against a tiny electric fire and waiting for the girl.

Though not for long. She knocked on the door and came silently in with a tray between her hands. She laid down the tray on a table and spoke just seven words, 'I hope this will be satisfactory, sir.'

Only seven, but enough for me to recognize her. Not by her face or her body or her way of speaking. Smith called her *girl* though she looked well over sixty. Not by the scar on her left cheek or the slight twitch between both her eyes. I'd never seen the damn woman before in my life, but I knew the type well. In spite of her years, the girl's rouge was too thick, her eyeshadow too heavy, and her lips smiled at me like lumps of red icing plastered on a cake. Mr Smith's maid-servant was an ex-pro, a former whore or a sometime gangster's moll, and I didn't like the look of her at all.

Nor did I like her next remark – not one little bit. 'Well, Billy,' the bitch said, with long scarlet fingernails hovering over the syphon and a jug of water. 'What's it to be? Aqua, or soda, or neat?'

'A little water please, but how did you know my first name, Miss?' I am aware that 'Miss' is a non-U form of address, but I couldn't think of anything else to say, and the obscene smile widened.

'That's an easy question,' she replied. 'I used to be paid to discover things about my customers, but your case was simple, Billy. You wrote William Easter down in Smith's register, so naturally I address you as Bill, though would you prefer Will, or Willie? My own name is Maggie.'

'Then, cheers, Miss May,' I said, taking the glass from her red claws, though not drinking its contents at once. Somehow I knew that Maggie May was a bad 'un, and I wanted to know a lot more about her. I also saw that there had been two glasses on the tray, and I nodded at the second one. 'Have a drink yourself, dear,' I said. 'Sit down and relax, my pretty one.'

'Thank you, Billy,' she replied. 'You are very kind, but they never allow me to drink on duty. Just a little soda to make the gentlemen feel relaxed and comfortable.' She raised the syphon but didn't point the nozzle at the glass. The nozzle was pointing at me when she pressed the trigger. 'Chin-chin,' she said, as the squirt of icy soda water caught me in the eyes, but I can't remember my reply. It was probably too vulgar to bear repetition. I was surprised and shocked and for a moment I was damn near blinded.

'Chin-chin,' the bitch repeated as I dabbed the liquid from my eyes. 'Here's to us – The Big Sleep, Billy. Farewell, my lovely.' Mindless quotations from the titles of Raymond Chandler, but there was nothing mindless about her face, and the thing in her hand was real enough. She'd dropped the syphon, and a short, stubby .32 revolver was trained on me. Like Dr Grace, I'd got hold of a bad psycho, and I tried to appeal to her better judgement.

'Don't shoot,' I said. 'Please put that gun away. I'm a friend. I never harmed you.' A useless appeal because the cow hadn't got a better judgement. She had no judgement at all, and her only response was a cackle of glee and another quote from Chandler. Quick thinking was needed and I'm pretty good on that score. The bitch thought she knew me, and I decided to play ball. 'Maggie,' I said. 'Please put that gun away. Maggie, I didn't recognize you. Maggie, I've come to take you home.' I flopped down on my knees and clutched the carpet. 'Home, Maggie. Let's go home.'

'Killer in the Rain,' she giggled and the gun muzzle came down against my bowed head. A fourth Chandler title, but there were more – plenty more, and my grip on the carpet tightened. You've all seen the trick done on old cinema screens. Looks simple, but it needs preparations. If the carpet is tacked down it won't work. If the floor is rough and uneven, the covering may not move and the victim will remain on his feet.

Victim? I was the victim. She had the gun and was running through the Chandler index. 'The Little Sister,' she whispered, and somehow it gave me courage. The Devil is said to quote scripture for his own ends, and though I'm not Satan, I do know Raymond Chandler.

The bitch had her back to the window, and the window was screened by curtains. I couldn't tell whether the window was closed or opened or how high it was from the ground. I could only pray, pray and tug, and I flexed my muscles and gave the rug a sudden heave.

It worked. That damned cinema gimmick really did work. The carpet shot forward, and Madam shot back. Back and out – out through The High Window and Into the Rain.

I didn't look down at her then. Not for a moment or two. I had a duty to perform first. I stood up, lifted my whisky glass and drank a toast to the immortal memory of Mr Raymond Chandler.

CHAPTER FOUR

'You, Bill. How cowardly – how disloyal – how completely selfish, can a man become?' After being questioned by the local police for hours, I'd finally been allowed to return to London, but no fatted calf was laid on. I reached Kirk's flat at six o'clock in the morning and found the old boy in a dark red dressing-gown and a hell of a temper.

'You tipped that woman through a window and she fell and broke her neck.' He banged the table so forcibly that I feared, or rather hoped, he might shatter one of his remaining fingers. 'Of course, she had a gun, but that was no excuse to kill her. Why didn't you merely disarm the bitch and grab the pistol out of her grasp? That's what I would have done. How any sane, responsible man would have acted!' Easy to say, but a vain boast, when her grasp was grasping the trigger. I considered I'd done extremely well and did not regret Miss May's death in the slightest.

'I'm sure that's true, Bill, but I regret her death.' He thumped the table again and coffee slopped from his cup. 'I regret Maggie's passing very much indeed, because she ties in with Tanek's murderer. Fortunate for you that she had a police record. Lucky that you had the sense to mention my name to the inspector. Strange that your car failed to start. The engine fired at once when a constable switched on the ignition.

'I suppose the battery is lodged in the engine compartment instead of the boot?' It was and I told him so, though I couldn't see how it mattered.

'Because the bonnet can be unlocked from the outside on those models, Bill.' He sipped his coffee and muttered something that sounded like, 'Damn little tin cars, only designed to potter around in Peckham.'

'Any schoolboy could have got at your battery, loosened a lead and replaced it as soon as you were comfortably installed at Mr Smith's boarding house.'

'You mean that it was a conspiracy – a plot to lure me into the house? That Smith was an accomplice?'

'Not Smith perhaps, but somebody was. Somebody wanted you to die, and he or she may have followed you from London. That's all I can say for sure, but we know one thing. The individual was quite certain that Miss May was bound to recognize you and take appropriate action, as she did.' He smiled slightly and pulled two sheets of typed paper out of his pocket. 'I said the woman had a record, and here's a synopsis of her misdeeds. Telephoned Scotland Yard as soon as I heard from the Southford inspector and they rushed it over here at once. Have a squint yourself, if you're interested.'

'Of course, I'm interested.' I reached out and took the pages from him. The first sheet had a photograph at the top, but it told me very little. A mug shot taken over thirty years ago, and time alters everyone.

'Elsie O'Mahoney – alias Coline Carlin – alias Maggie May,' read the print beneath the face, and I knew I'd been right about its owner. Maggie May had been born in Liverpool, 1920, and she'd drifted to London at the age of seventeen. Waitress in a café, dancehall hostess, professional criminal. The old, old story, though why tarts should be regarded as crooks is beyond me.

But, ah yes – one tart should have been. Miss May was only twenty-one when she pinched a chap's wallet. Up before the magistrates and case dismissed through lack of evidence. Only twenty-two when she planted a dart through another chap's eye. Self defence was the verdict and she was bound over to keep the peace. She kept it until the eighth month started and a benevolent protector came on the scene: Bruno Kremer.

Bruno the Bastard, as he liked to be called, must have been quite a young man in those days. An eager, ambitious young man just starting to build an empire of vice and crime, and he must have found Miss May excellent building material. Prostitution to begin with, but just as a beginning. Blackmail and extortion were Bruno's specialities, and Maggie May became an expert assistant in both fields. Manageress of a night club which was also a brothel for the better type of client. Clients who never knew they had been photographed during their activities, till Mr Kremer applied the squeeze.

But one client suspected and he informed the law. Mr X, as the Yard called him, went back to the scene of his activities, and a couple of rozzers followed him through the rear door. They found Miss May taking shots with a camera, behind a see-through mirror, and they attempted to arrest her, but she got in first. Five shots from a revolver similar to the one which had threatened me foiled the attempt and ruined two promising careers. Maggie made off from the Scouse, but they got her after six weeks. They usually do, and the charges were attempted murder, grievous bodily harm and extorting money on threat of libel, exposure or prosecution.

Maggie went behind bars for a long time, but not long enough. After five years she was certified as insane and transferred to a mental asylum. A month later, she was free.

'Scotland Yard couldn't commit themselves, Bill, but it seems likely Bruno Kremer arranged her escape and fixed her up with forged papers.' Kirk's voice interrupted my reading material. 'Maybe there really is honour amongst thieves. Maybe he was frightened she might talk. Perhaps he was in love with the blasted woman. All we know for sure is that she slaved away for Mr Smith ever since, and she'd probably still be slaving there if you hadn't gone and killed her.'

'Why did she pick on me?' I asked, but I already knew the answer: revenge. Bruno Kremer hired me as his bodyguard and got a bullet through his bloody body. I'm not admitting that I put it there, but a lot of people thought that was the case, and if the woman shared those suspicions . . .

Revenge – no. I refused to accept that that was the bitch's motive. If you want to avenge somebody, you repeat the injured party's name while pointing a gun at the injurer. Miss May, or whatever she called herself while working for Smith, hadn't repeated any proper names at all. She'd only quoted titles from Raymond Chandler before I shoved her through The High Window.

But Maggie May had been sent to a lunatic asylum, and I'd come from one, before she met me. Somehow, someone had tampered with my car's ignition and forced me to seek sanctuary and food at Smith's chilly establishment. Lunacy was to blame, and maniacs squatting on the moon must be responsible. I felt crazy myself. I was also damned tired and half asleep. I just wanted to close my eyes and rest for a moment.

'Not yet, Bill.' Either I'd spoken aloud or Kirk possessed the gift of thought-reading. 'I have also been up most of the night, and though far older than you, I am still fit and eager for the fray, so listen carefully.

'I can give you a bed in a moment, but listen and look at me.' I did look, and what I saw was most displeasing. The general's face looked as red as his vulgar dressing-gown. 'What you have told me proves you are a cowardly liar, but it shows something else. Maybe a way to the truth.' He cleared his throat and knocked back the dregs in his coffee cup. 'One madman killed himself, and a female maniac was killed by you. But I am quite sure that they were both creations of little Tom Ryde. And here is my news.' He lowered the cup and reached for his cigar case. 'Tommy has a descendant: a daughter.'

CHAPTER FIVE

I never received much formal education. Got flung out of an eminent public school at the age of seventeen and was sent down from Balliol two years later. But I still wore an Oxford tie. I had a paper in my pocket to show I was on official, government business. I can talk like a gentleman when the need arises.

'You bloody, flaming louts.' The need arose as soon as I parked my car in Carthage Road School. A football thudded against the roof, and I hurried out to deal with the louts responsible. 'Yes, you son. I'm talking to you.' I grabbed one of the louts by the hair and kneed him hard in the balls. 'That hurts, doesn't it, but not as much as the next one will.' My knee came up again and the ape yelped in anguish as it connected. 'Yes, very painful, but I'm going to tell you a secret. If you want trouble, I come from the place where it's made. A load of trouble, you bleedin', fuckin' pack of bastards.' I flexed my muscles and he toppled against a second and slightly bigger bastard, who promptly fell down on his arse. I planted my right shoe on his wrist and pressed hard.

'Well, boys and girls, I think we understand each other, and anyone who lays a hand or a football on my car again is welcome to try. He or she will pay through the nail. Pay to the last – the uttermost farthing.

'Now, will one of you, young ladies and gentlemen, be kind enough to take me to your headmaster?' I smiled pleasantly but the six brutish faces remained blank, though the two I had disciplined were sobbing loudly. 'The headmaster,' I repeated. 'This is a school, even though it's comprehensive. A notice on the gates states that I have come to the right address, and there must be a headmaster on the premises. I wish to speak to him and will be most obliged if you will show me the way towards his office.' I still smiled but applied more foot pressure at the same time. 'The headmaster, please.'

'Headmaster . . .' A cowlike creature of indeterminate sex finally responded. 'You mean Tony Wolfe, the Community Leader.'

'Yes, Mr Anthony Wolfe. That is the name. How stupid of me to forget it, but don't any of you continue to be stupid. Touch that car and I'll crush off all your bleedin' fingers. Now lead me to Mr Wolfe's office, my dear.'

I bowed to the human cow and followed its steps across the playground. I had heard or read about Mr Anthony Wolfe, as it happened, and his name raised praise or fury depending on one's point of view. Mr Wolfe was a local councillor as well as being a headmaster, though he omitted the second title and called himself Community Leader, which is OK, providing you've got a community who are prepared to be led. Mr Wolfe hadn't and Carthage Road was a school in name only. A dump, a breeding ground for crime, illiteracy and all the rest of our squalid ills. I could smell the atmosphere of the place like sewage gas being compressed into a solid. Hear it through the doors of the unruly classrooms. Sense defeat as though on a battlefield. One war had been lost forever, and who was responsible? Where did the blame lie? I hadn't a clue, but I was soon to find out. My escort had halted before a door labelled 'Community Leader Wolfe – Do Not Knock – Please Enter.' A damned silly notice to put up in any school, but I followed its instructions and barged straight into the sanctum, though I didn't find sanctuary. The room was crowded with more unwashed louts and loutesses, and they were all making a bloody din.

'Gibber – gibber – gibber,' muttered one male specimen. 'Weren't my fault, Tony,' said another. 'Yer can't blame us, Tone,' pleaded two female exhibits.

'*Halt's Maul*,' I yelled in my best German and putting all my strength behind it. 'That means silence, so shut your fuckin' mouths, or I'll fuckin' quick sew 'em up for fuckin' ever.' That is the only kind of language such scum understand, and mercifully the orders were obeyed. 'Now, *Raus*. Out. Get out of this bloody room immediately.' I eyed the brutes like the brutes they were as they sidled past me, and only had to answer a single question.

'What? You do not know whom I am, my boy. Nobody has informed you.' I glanced at a dishevelled adult figure seated beside a desk. 'Well, I shall tell you, so that there will be no further lack of knowledge, my boy.

'My name, Uncle Tom, is Dr William Easter, and I hold the post of a Senior Inspector of Schools.' My glower was transferred to the black face of my questioner. 'That gives me the power to close this school – establishment – menagerie, with a single signature, and close it I will, Rastus. Yes, Carthage Road will be shut forever, unless you are out of this room within two seconds flat.' I gave his thick scalp a sharp rap to speed him on his way, and then turned to my host. 'Well, Mr Wolfe,' I said. 'I am waiting for an explanation, so please provide one.' I flashed the pass that Kirk or one of his former buddies at Army Intelligence had provided and was glad to see him wince.

Mr Wolfe didn't look like a wolf or even a wolf in sheep's clothing. He looked like a ruddy sheep of a man, and his voice had a sheepish bleat.

'I'm sorry, Dr Easter,' he said. 'We are all very pleased to see you, of course, but didn't expect you today. No, not today. The last day of the term, and the summer holidays start tomorrow. Everything is a bit chaotic at the moment, but . . .'

'But what, Community Leader?' The sheep had broken off with a stammer and I prompted him. 'Aren't things always chaotic at Carthage Road? The police and the public say that they are, and my fellow inspectors share that view.

'Crime and vandalism, Mr Wolfe.' I don't know why I pulled out an empty notebook and invented a list of charges. There was no need for it. All I needed to do was to ask the man a simple question, but maybe I enjoyed baiting him. 'Yes, three cases of mugging last month, four of larceny, five of petty thefts from the supermarkets, ten of violence at football matches, countless cases of hooliganism on buses and the underground.

'The list is too long to repeat, but the crimes all started here, Mr Community Leader. At Carthage Road Sewage Farm, and they've got to stop. You must stop them, Mr Wolfe. You draw a headmaster's salary, and the responsibility is yours. Yours alone, sir. And the discipline and educational standards of this school must be tightened up. Why, in all my years as one of Her Majesty's Inspectors, I have never witnessed such bear-garden behaviour, and it will end during the first week of next term.' The sheep was on the verge of tears and I decided to end the performance. 'Now, I wish to visit Mrs Bloom, who is in charge of Domestic Science, so please direct me to her room.

'No, I'll find my own way, thank you. Turn left and the fourth door on the right, you said.' I pushed away the notebook and bowed grimly. 'And don't worry, Mr Wolfe. We shall meet again after the end of the holidays.'

I almost said on the Ides of March, but checked myself in time and strode out. Out into chaos again. A jungleland of children swarming in the corridors. The voices of teachers trying to restore order and failing. Mr Wolfe had a lot to answer for, and I almost wished I was a proper inspector, till I reached the fourth door and pushed it open.

Silence! Complete silence apart from the whirr of drills and sewing machines. I couldn't believe my eyes or ears for a moment and then realized it was true. The Domestic Science class was hard at work and they seemed happy to be working. Thirty to forty boys and girls were assembling electrical parts, sewing skirts and pressing other garments. And they were obviously contented and proud of their toil; that was the strange thing. Not a single face looked up at me or even noticed that I was in the room. The same brutish faces that I'd encountered outside. I felt that I must be in another world, till one of the toilers raised her hand.

'Please, Missus,' she said, speaking in broad, nasal cockney. 'Sorry to disturb you, but me and Mavis is out of thread.' A voice answered, but I didn't see its owner for a moment. Her face was screened by a copy of the *Daily Globe*. 'Then fetch some more and be smart about it, girl. Be very sharp, Cynthia. We are under contract to finish that assignment on time and there's a penalty clause. Mrs Cohen wants her work completed by five o'clock this afternoon at the latest.

'And you, boy. Yes, I'm talking to you, Peter Bloggs. Have you forgotten the price of solder?' The newspaper was lowered and I saw the face of the woman I had come to meet.

Molly Bloom was in her late twenties, and she had long blonde hair. That tells you very little, but Ryde's daughter was just about the most beautiful human female I'd ever clapped eyes on.

'Oh, Peter, don't slop the stuff around so lavishly,' she said. 'Lazarus and Line pay well for good work, but they expect value for money and we must see they get it. Don't waste materials, my boy. Just dab the joints gently. Though firmly, of course.' She turned and saw me. Her blue eyes smiled. 'Can I help you, sir?'

'I hope so, Mrs Bloom, but tell me something first.' I looked at the industrious toilers with something akin to awe. 'How the hell do you do it?'

'Do what? Mr . . . Thank you, Dr Easter, but I'm not sure exactly what you mean.' I explained my problem and Mrs Bloom closed one eye and winked. 'Surely that's obvious, and the answer is £sd; the root of all evil; the source of all endeavour. This bunch and all the other brainless oafs who come here are on piece-work, and they get paid for their labours. Well paid, providing that the work is satisfactory and delivered on time, Bobby Brown!' She raised her voice and pointed at a small black boy wielding a file. 'Tony Wolfe told me that an Inspector of Schools was coming to Carthage Road, Mr Easter, and this might be described as a school, if it had a headmaster to run it, and pupils capable of absorbing education.

'But we haven't got either, have we, Dora Wright?' Her pointing finger moved to an extremely fat girl busily sewing away at the back of the class. 'These kids want to work, Mr Easter, but they like to be paid for their labours, and I pay 'em. Anything wrong about that?'

'No, not in my view, Mrs Bloom, but a slightly unorthodox method of teaching, perhaps.' That's what I said, but my admiration rose like a pressure gauge, because I knew what she was up to, and it was a damn good thing.

Every small employer wants labour, providing it's industrious and cheap, and Mrs Bloom supplied the labourers. Very few dim-witted kids want to be educated, but they all like money, and so does everybody else. Mrs Bloom fulfilled two needs at once. She was not only one of the most attractive women I'd ever met, she was a bloody genius, and I felt like hugging her then and there.

'How much do you get?' I asked and got a straight answer.

'Far too little, Mr Easter. Only half the net profits, less breakages and less delays. Mere chicken feed compared to what I do for them and the community.' She moved to the window and I followed her. She looked out at the playground and the car park, and pointed at my car. She shook her head and clicked her tongue.

'I hope you're enjoying this lesson, and approve of my ideas on education, Mr Easter, if that is your real name, which I doubt. I doubt very much indeed, and you can surely guess why.

'Oh no, don't bother to show me any forged documents, please.' I had reached in my pocket to produce old Kirk's phoney pass, but she gave my hand a sharp rap with a ruler. 'They probably impressed Tony Wolfe, but they won't fool me. I watched you arrive, Mr Easter, and you don't look like an inspector of education. Certainly you didn't behave like one. How wicked to knee poor little Terry Triggs in the crotch. Might have hurt him badly and ruined our assembly lines.

'Just an ordinary, fun-loving boy, playing with a football. Such a shame that it happened to hit your not very smart car, by accident. Such a vile reprisal to make; callous and cruel and vicious.' She paused and I heard a bell ring in the distance. I also heard the sound of several disordered classes breaking up, but the assembly line didn't budge. Mrs Bloom's Domestic Science class worked on, regardless. 'Overtime, now. Double pay for the next hour, but no slacking, remember. And no talking, Marion Porridge.' Mrs Bloom raised her voice to address the toilers, and then grinned at me. 'Well, Mr Easter, or whatever you're actually called, what do you want? We've established that you're not an HMI or even a Divisional Inspector, but some kind of cheap crook with sadistic tendencies, so please state your business and be done with it.

'Private.' She opened her eyes wide as I made the request. 'We're private enough in here. That bunch are completely hooked on their work. Brainwashed by the thought of double pay, and they won't hear a word till the job's completed.

'Oh, very well.' She watched my expression and shrugged her shoulders before turning to the bunch. 'Now listen to me, you lot. Mrs Cohen and Messrs Lazarus and Line will be along to settle up at five o'clock sharp, so put your backs into the work. And your brains, such as they are, Peter M'Turk. Concentrate on pleasing our customers and nothing else. This gentleman and I are going into the staff room across the corridor, and every word of stupid chatter I hear will cost the class a pound of their cut.

'Every *single* whisper, Peter, and don't forget that.' She opened the door and waved me through. 'A hundred pence per whisper, boys and girls. Keep that in mind, and don't let it slip from your memories.' She strode out of the room and motioned me to follow her to another room. A small and completely empty room, apart from the furniture; lockers on one wall, a dartboard on the other. A timetable facing the board, and a general air of hopelessness and defeat.

'Quiet enough for you, Mr Inspector of Schools?' she said, sitting down before a long baize-covered table. 'Secretive enough, Dr Easter? The defeated armies have fled to Dartmoor or the Costa Brava to lick their scars of battle, and we are quite alone. So speak. Have a chair. Tell me your business.'

'First, I'd like to say that you're a bloody fine teacher, Mrs Bloom.' Courtesy costs nothing and I felt that compliments were in order, but in this case they didn't work. Mrs Bloom merely nodded rather smugly. She knew she was bloody fine – one of the best.

'But my next point is more personal, I'm afraid.' I lowered myself into a hard-backed chair. 'In 1979 you were married to a man, Leopold Bloom, who died six months later, after a motor accident.' She nodded a second time, though not quite so smugly, and I continued. 'But what was your original name? How were you called before Leopold came on the scene, Molly Bloom?'

'Good,' she said. 'Almost very good. The straightforward, honest, manly approach. Usually, they beat about the bush, but I much prefer your method.' She opened her handbag and took out a packet of cigarettes. 'The question is, *How much?*'

'Sorry, but I'm not with you,' I said with all honesty. 'How much for what?'

'For the interview, the story, of course, Mr Easter. I'm still news, though it all happened a long time ago.' She looked at me as though I was one of the dimmer denizens of her class and lit a cigarette. 'How much will your editor pay for the exclusive rights? I can even supply the title: *A Tale of Treason, as Told by a Survivor, the Late Miss Molly Ryde.*

'Nothing, Mr Easter, and you're not a reporter, but some kind of Secret Service wallah?' I'd repeated Kirk's mendacious story and she frowned sadly. 'Very well, have it for free, if you must, though I don't know why, or what I can tell you.' She paused to pull at the cigarette. 'Yes, I'm Tommy Ryde's survivor, and my mother was a maid working at the vicarage before I was born.

'Born out of wedlock, but I was given Dad's name as a sort of memento, though I'm not sure why. I was in my teens when Mum died. That was July 1976; over thirty years since Tom defected to the Nazis.' Though I found the dates rather puzzling, I didn't try to stop her and she continued. 'And Tommy Ryde was good in a squalid way, Mr Easter. I never met him, of course, but I've heard recordings of his broadcasts and they sounded very good. Far more effective than William Joyce, Baillie-Stuart or John Amery. They made the British people laugh, and laughter is a sort of tonic in wartime. But nobody laughed at Tommy Ryde.

'And you can't pay me a penny, Mr Easter? How mean your employer must be. What exactly do you want? My story is old hat and in the history books. Tom Ryde died about the same time as Hitler, but I'm alive, so what the hell can I tell you?'

'Matter of National Security, Molly Bloom.' Kirk had provided two faked passes, and I reached for the second, which was lodged in my hip pocket, with a fish hook sewn alongside it for protection. It took me about a quarter of a minute to reach the card and when I tried to draw it out, the damned hook caught me.

'Bastard – bloody stupid old bastard,' I yelped. The stitching came away and my hand came out with a Glossop's 'marble-blue, salmon-type' special firmly attached to the index finger. 'You said that my boss was a mean-minded miser, Molly, and you were right. He is also an interfering, senile dotard, a gruesome, geriatric ghoul.' I still kept abusing my benefactor as the blood dribbled onto the table, and the card fell to the floor.

'What on earth are you doing Mr Easter?' Mrs Bloom had seen my distress and took immediate action. 'An angler's hook with the barb imbedded through one of your middle fingers. How very odd, and quite deeply imbedded! Must get it out, but not to worry. There's a first aid kit over there somewhere with a scalpel and bandages.' She stood up, fetched the kit and produced the scalpel. I saw the steel glint and then closed my eyes for a moment. 'Good – good boy. Keep very still, and here – goes,' she said as the blade bit into my flesh. I must have screeched like a kitten. But when I looked at it, I saw that Molly Bloom had done a fair repair job. Glossop's 'marble-blue' lay on the table top, and she was dabbing plaster over my wound. 'Are you a very keen angler, Mr Easter?' she asked. 'Really fanatical. Mad enough to carry your gear around in a hip pocket. How rash and dangerous, and foolhardy!' She still held the scalpel, and I kept still for an obvious reason. The tip was pressing against my throat, and my pass – Kirk's phoney identification card – was in Molly's free hand. 'But this is highly entertaining, Bill. Really spectacular stuff, though doubtless you know the contents by heart already. Listen to your life history as addressed to whom it may concern and signed by the Foreign Secretary and the representative of something called HAIR 2, though I don't know what that means.' Somehow she managed to read the card and keep the little knife firmly in position.

'You are a captain, Billy Boy. Not of thousands, or of legions, or of hosts, but a genuine captain in the British Army, and acting in the interests of British Army Intelligence. Grade One – Serial Number XK 10 R. To be thoroughly trusted and relied on, absolutely in defence of the Queen and the subjugation of her enemies.

'How nice and reassuring that sounds, but how puny you look

with a knife against your Adam's apple, Bill dear. Most pathetic and sad and vulnerable.'

'Wrong, Molly,' I said, and I meant what I said, because I wasn't vulnerable. The scalpel was no longer against my throat, but in my right hand. While she had been sneering at Kirk's inventions and those of his colleague, Colonel Basil Collarbone, the present head of a military intelligence unit known as HAIR, my fingers had crept towards her and grabbed the offensive weapon. I was quite safe from Madam Bloom at the moment, but . . .

I don't know why, but I told her everything. I bared my soul and made a clean breast, as they put it. I mentioned Kirk's attempts at blackmail and how bloody successful they had been. I spoke of his obsession with her father and what a bloody fool he was, but I never finished – never got a chance. Molly stared at me as though she was looking at a ghost – a darned objectionable one.

'My father, Bill?' she said. 'Thomas Ryde defected in 1944, which would make me about thirty-nine by now. Do I look as old and decrepit as that?'

'No,' I replied, which was the truth, though I was almost forty myself and didn't care for the word 'decrepit'. 'I'd put you at about twenty-eight. I suppose the old fool has made a hash of things as usual.'

'Correct, Bill. I will be twenty-eight next birthday. But your General Kirk is not entirely wrong. I am Ryde's sole surviving relative – he had a brother.'

It was the first time I'd heard of that, but Molly soon put me in the picture, and it was a somewhat dirty one. The Rt Revd Mr Ryde and his missus had produced two sons, named Tom and Terry. Terry was the younger of the two by three years, and he worshipped his older brother. 'Obsessed' was the expression Molly used or maybe 'mesmerized by', but it didn't matter. Terry was under Tom's thumb and thought of him as a sort of Christ figure. Well, like Christ, Tom left a legacy.

Not a gift I'd have fancied myself, of course. Soiled goods – second hand, discarded clothing might be apt descriptions for Uncle Tom's legacy. Her name was Annie Craine, her age was seventeen, she was gainfully employed as a maid at the vicarage. She also shared Tom, the young master's bed, in her off-duty hours. Terry's obsession increased.

'No, not jealousy, Bill.' Molly shook her head at my question. 'One can't be jealous of a god, but eat the scraps that fall from his table.'

So when Tom departed to fresh fields and pastures new, Terry popped the question and Annie responded. An unlawful union and not a happy one, though its fruit was Molly. Its conversation ran on one line: Thomas Ryde.

'Terry and Annie were my parents, Bill, and they hardly discussed anybody else except Uncle Tommy. When I was eighteen and got into a training college, they fell off a cliff in North Wales and were killed instantly. An accident perhaps – or joint suicide. I do not know. I have no idea, but I'm quite sure about this.' Molly paused and stood up. 'When their bodies hit the scree, they were both thinking about Uncle Tom.'

'How can you be so certain about that?' An obvious enquiry to my mind, but I didn't get a straight answer. All I received was a load of meaningless, spookish twaddle, which told me seven-eighths of nine-tenths of F-all.

'I think that your General Kirk could just be right, Bill,' Molly said, moving away from me towards the lockers again. 'Mummy didn't think that Tommy Ryde could die. How could he when the man wasn't a person at all, but just a fleeting presence full of blight?' She misquoted deliberately and grinned. 'Mummy was only a girl when Tom laid her, and I don't think she loved him. Not in an adoring adolescent way, that is. I honestly believe that she felt herself a chattel, and my father did the same. That's why they got together, and God, it was a rotten partnership. Can the owner of two human souls ever be destroyed, Bill? Has anybody got the power to tame a devil?' Molly had reached the lockers, but mercifully she didn't reach for a second knife. She opened another door beside the first and smiled. 'May I offer you a drink, Bill, though I'm sorry we have only whisky and gin.'

I told her that a drop of Scotch would be just the ticket, and she poured it out, mixed herself a gin and tonic and brought over the glasses.

'Cheers, Bill,' she said, taking a sip and smiling. 'Bill – William Easter; what a pleasant name for such an abominable man. A man who impersonates an Inspector of Schools and knocks school children about. Who pretends to be a secret agent and guards his credentials with fish hooks. Very bad, quite atrocious, but basically on the side of the angels, I believe. You can't understand the mind of a man like Tommy Ryde, a maker of monsters who tortured souls for fun.' She picked up her cigarette from an ashtray and leaned forward. 'Do you ever think about the soul, Bill?'

'Yes,' I said, but I wasn't thinking about it at that moment. I was contemplating Molly's lips and her breasts and something old Kirk had mentioned not long ago. Just an incident, a trick of memory, but I could imagine the scene quite clearly. Ryde's parents, the respected clergyman and his wife, taking tea in the vicarage. Ryde's mistress, a girl in a maid's uniform, pouring out their tea and preparing to leave when one of them had called her back. 'Annie, please switch on the radio, and turn to Lord Haw-Haw.'

So the girl had twisted a knob and adjusted the wave length, and they all heard a voice they recognized. A man's voice, though not the harsh, hectoring tones of William Joyce. The man spoke softly, pleadingly, and his voice was almost hypnotic. 'Good evening, ladies and gentlemen,' he had said. 'Before reading the news, I think I should introduce myself. My name is Second Lieutenant Thomas Ryde, and I am talking to you from Germany.'

So the parents had sat and listened to their older son. Probably they had tried to reassure themselves at the beginning. 'Not Tommy – Just Nazi propaganda – An imposter – All lies – Our Tommy, our son, wouldn't – couldn't have done such a thing.' Then at last they had reached their final conclusion and drunk the cup of despair. 'But my God – he has!'

Poor parents – poor girl – poor dear Molly Bloom. She had stubbed out the cigarette and I raised my arms and pulled her towards me. Our lips were just about to meet when . . .

'Cor! Stone the crows,' said the first male voice. 'Up and at 'er,' remarked a second, even more heartily. 'And in a place of public education – How ruddy disgusting.' The third speaker sounded female, and her words showed deep disapproval. I released Molly and looked at our visitors: two thin men in overalls and a fat woman in a fur coat. The school had closed for the summer holidays, and apart from ourselves and the Domestic Science class, the building should have been empty. So who had interrupted us? A clock struck five, the fat woman patted her fat handbag and the penny dropped.

Domestic Science! Mrs Cohen and Messrs Lazarus and Line had called to inspect their goods and take delivery.

CHAPTER SIX

'Well, Bill, better late than never, I suppose, but one would have thought . . .' I had reported progress to Kirk and he wasn't pleased. He looked bloody annoyed and eyed his watch coldly. 'Almost twenty-four hours have passed since you met that woman, so what the hell kept you?'

'Gaining her confidence, General,' I said, which was true up to a point. Chit-chat in a pub, flattery in a restaurant, and culmination in a hotel bedroom. A very pleasant way of passing the time, and we'd slept late. Why not? Molly had a long holiday and I was on expenses. Kirk's filthy lucre had settled the bill.

'You fornicator, Bill. You filthy, bloody adulterator, but we'll say no more about that.' Generous of the old boy, I thought, but what can one say when a *fait* is *accompli*? 'Well, what did you learn from Mrs Bloom, Billy? Was there a family likeness?'

'I never knew her family, General Kirk, but I can say this: Molly Bloom is obsessed with the story of Tom Ryde.' I tried to explain her obsession and I probably failed: 'haunted' might have been a better word. Molly seemed quite convinced that her uncle was still alive. She was frightened of him and terrified that he might return one day. She might deplore what he had done and curse his name, but she used it. Even when she was asleep, her voice mentioned him. Ryde – Tommy Ryde – Tommy Ryde. 'Come back to me, Tommy.'

'Sounds batty to my mind, but that could be to our advantage.' Kirk glanced at a copy of the *Daily Globe*. 'Heard the news, son? Erik Brenner is due out tomorrow.'

'I thought everybody knew that, but what about him?' I took the paper and looked at a picture on the first page. The face of a young man in a black uniform addressing a crowd. The face would not be young today, and the photograph had been taken a long time ago. The man was nearly ninety now and almost half his life had been spent in prison.

'You are being very dull and boring, Bill, and surely it's obvious.' Kirk paused to blow his nose and open a cigar case. 'Erik Brenner is the last top Nazi still in prison. The last inmate of Spandau Castle. The only German who actually knew Ryde and worked with him in the Third Reich. Don't you think we should have a chat with him?'

'By all means, General,' I said. 'Yes, indeed, and you are obviously the right man for the job. Brenner's opposite number in fact. A former British Intelligence boss, and the same age group. Former buddies, in fact, and you'll get on like houses on fire.'

'Don't be impertinent, Bill Easter.' Kirk had lit his cigar, and he glowered at me while he sucked the end. 'Erik Brenner is no buddy of mine, but just about the worst enemy that I or this country have ever had. I have tried to talk to him. For almost two weeks I interviewed Brenner after he surrendered, and I got no change out of the bastard. He wouldn't even mention Tom Ryde. He said nothing at all.

'No, Billy Boy. The ex-Gauleiter of Essen won't say a word to me, and I can't blame him for that. My testimony at Nuremberg probably helped to get him his life sentence, and there are no regrets on my part.

'But you, Bill.' Kirk closed his eyes in an effort of concentration. 'No, not you. I don't think you'd be more successful, but I wonder, just wonder. I wonder whether the former minister might not let down his hair for Mrs Bloom.'

* * *

As we came towards it, I remembered the city, and why not? I must have visited Berlin half a dozen times in as many years, and I pointed out some places of interest to Molly. The long road, as straight as an arrow, the loom of the Wannsee Lakes, which the bomb-aimers had used as markers during the war, and a tiny line in the distance – The Wall. 'For East is East and West is West, and never the twain shall meet.' I think I quoted a bit of Kipling, but I can't be sure because the pilot was making his final approach. He wheeled slightly, whilst crossing the *Funkturm*, and began the sweep across Charlottenburg, towards the dark rectangle which was Tempelhof.

I kept glancing at Molly on the seat beside me as we started the last descent. I thought that I loved her, but another emotion kept rearing its ugly head – bewilderment.

I hadn't been able to scratch the surface of what Molly Bloom really was. I knew that I liked her, and judging by her love-making, I felt – no, I was sure – that she fancied me. But beneath the cynicism and the affection, there was another self which I couldn't share. A lonely, haunted ego, shut away and completely self-contained. Waiting, perhaps. Waiting for the same thing as Charlie Kirk. News of Tommy Ryde – the boy who had gone away.

'How many times was Uncle Tom's voice transmitted from there?' she asked, staring down at the Radio Tower. Her voice was sad and bitter till we were told to put on seat belts and it altered.

'Nice to travel on an expense account,' she remarked. 'General Kirk seems a generous employer. I mean financially, of course.'

'You know what Kirk is, Molly.' I'd seen the little bitch wink and grinned back at her. 'But do you know – really know – what you're being paid to do?'

'How to deal with Herr Erik Brenner, you mean. I should do, after the way you and Kirk prepared me. In any case, it's too late for any improvement now, and here we are.'

The wheels slammed the tarmac in a harsh, screaming rush, and the big BEA plane seemed to shoot forward, slowed, wheeled and drew up before the main immigration hall. We joined the line of passengers and as I walked down the ramp, I smelled Berlin: a difficult odour to describe. Petrol, human sweat, cigar smoke and something else which shouldn't be there. Still drifting from the East Sector came the acid reek of rubble.

'Langner!' Kirk had promised we would be met, and his contact took my hand in a firm, manly grip and then, to her obvious delight, stooped and kissed Molly's. Hans Langner had a short, trim beard, stood well over six foot tall and probably tipped the scales at around sixteen stone, most of 'em bone and muscle. He resembled a benevolent ogre invented by one of the Brothers Grimm or some similar characters. His appearance was slightly marred by his dress, or rather the lack of it. Herr Langner had an open-necked collar, a black leather jerkin and a pair of red plastic shorts.

'*Servus*, Herr Easter,' he boomed. 'Welcome to West Berlin, Miss Bloom. Please come with me, dear friends.' Despite his clothes and his tendency to shout, Langner was clearly a person of authority. He flicked his vast fingers at a group of custom officers, immigration officials and policemen and they stepped aside. A porter hurried to take our bags, and within seconds we were tucked into the back of a chauffeur-driven limousine. 'I would have liked to have offered you a drink, first, but unfortunately, there is no time. He consulted his watch and then rapped the driver's partition. '*Schnell, Franz. Zu Spandau.*

'Yes, your flight was ten minutes late, Herr Easter.' He spoke in English again. 'A great pity, but we must hurry. The ceremony is due to start at four o'clock sharp.'

'Ceremony?' The car had moved off and I tried to edge away from Langner's bare legs, which were covered with blond, downy hair. 'Sorry, but I'm not with you, old boy.'

'Then perhaps "celebration" would be a better term, Herr Easter. A gala to mark the release of one of the great martyrs for the National Socialist Partie.' Though his English was pretty faultless, he slipped a bit over the word 'party'. 'Yes, a martyr indeed, *mein Herr*. Erik Brenner, *Standartenführer SS*. Former Gauleiter of Essen – former Chief Organizer of all broadcasting, and answerable only to Dr Joseph Goebbels himself. Sometime officer in charge of all labour camps in the Ukraine. One of the first men to be framed by your unjust War Crimes' Tribunal in Nuremberg, and wickedly condemned by your judges. The last prisoner to be released from the captivity of your soldiers in Spandau and your Bolshevik allies.'

'*Your!*' I didn't like the repetition of that pronoun, and I didn't care for Herr Hans Langner either. I was about to tell the ruddy Kraut that I'd not been born when the war ended, but I wasn't given the chance. Molly interrupted.

'You consider that the court at Nuremberg was unjust, Herr Langner?' she asked. 'The sentence too heavy?'

'Heavy!' Her enquiry made Langner look slightly put out, if not extremely angry. 'My father was a regular soldier and a colonel in the German Army, Miss Bloom. A man of the 20th of July – hanged by piano wire, under the orders of Erik Brenner in person – the bastard!'

'My mother,' the ogre continued, choking back a sob, 'Mutti, sold herself to American soldiers, after the collapse. Sold her flesh, to keep us in food, and some of those soldiers were black. Black animals, Herr Easter.' We were rounding the Kaiser Wilhelm Memorial Church, still preserved as a monument to pain, and he broke off . . . out of sorrow for his darling Mutti, probably, though I didn't share his feelings. Mutti had obviously lorded it during the Dritte Reich. Gorged herself on French food and drink, and soaked her body in French perfume. Mutti probably had had a couple of Slavs to slave for her, and she'd smiled at the thought of the Jews in concentration camps. Mutti was a right old bitch and good luck to our honest soldiers, black, white or khaki. The lads had earned a bit of fun, and let's hope that Mutti, Muttchen, Frau Langner gave 'em good value.

'No, not heavy, Mrs Bloom.' I was just about to voice my opinion when Langner resumed his discourse. 'Not nearly heavy enough, and I apologise for quoting the views of a few of our *Lumpenproletariat*. That's what Marx called the young swine, and he was right. Waste disposers and eaters of waste. Handlers of rubbish and spreaders of garbage.

'A man commits a crime and gets locked up. Quite fair, providing the sentence is as long as the crime, and in Brenner's case that should have been death. Death by hanging – by torture – by disembowelment – his head paraded through Germany in an iron cage.

'However, that man will soon be free, and we will witness his release in approximately half an hour, so let's forget the past and talk about the present.' He pressed himself comfortably against the cushions, and his hairy leg pressed against mine. 'Tell me, Mr Easter, how is your General Kirk? In good health, I hope.'

'Excellent!' I'd said that the Major General was in fair running order for his age and Langner smiled. 'My own Chief was sorry that he couldn't meet you himself, but for obvious reasons that seemed undesirable. I myself have little knowledge about your business, and you must think of me as a courier, a sort of guide. I can provide tickets for you to visit the Hotel Frankreich, where they are holding a party in the beast's honour, but once there, you will be on your own.' He turned away from me and looked at Molly, as the driver crossed the Zoo intersection. 'Miss Bloom, how much do you know about the Reichminister?'

'What everyone else knows,' Molly replied, staring out of the window. We were in the Ost-West Axis now, the road running straight ahead, passing the Winged Victory statue, with its French gun-barrels glittering in the sunlight and the slightly comic angel looking down on us. 'What I have read in books and newspapers and heard on the television and radio. All general knowledge, apart from Kirk's briefing.'

'Which should have been very thorough, I imagine.' Langner followed her gaze through the window. Reichkanzlerplatz, Reichstrasse, a brief glimpse of the Olympic Stadium and, at last, Spandauerdamm and the Castle.

The Castle looked exactly what a prison should look like. It crouched, low and gaunt, with decorative towers and a studded gate, and resembled a pretentious version of Wandsworth Jail, but this jail had a difference. Spandau Castle was on holiday.

The police guards and British troops stationed before the gate looked very smart in their grey and khaki uniforms, but their faces were sad and lonely as they watched the crowd before them. Though I couldn't see what they had to be frightened of – not then.

Apart from a cluster of reporters beside the gate, the men and women were mainly old. Old, but not all decrepit, though some bore the scars of battle and lacked arms or legs or other organs. That didn't worry me in the slightest. What could an army of dotards do against well-drilled troops and rozzers, I thought, and then the truth came and fear joined it. The crowd was not just a group come to cheer a man or watch a spectacle. It was too quiet and too well ordered. Every member was reliving past glories and praying that Erik Brenner might revive 'em. *Der Führer ist tot – Heil der Führer.*

I apologise if I'm boring you. Imagination running away possibly, but somebody once said that the Germans were a race of carnivorous sheep, and there were the sheep, thirsting for blood in front of me. I didn't realize that the car had stopped till I felt Langner tap my knee. He asked us to follow him.

We were outside a little café facing the prison, and gay with blue-painted tables and striped sunshades. He led us through the crowded bar and up a staircase to the first floor and opened a door. The room inside was very clean and neat, with three chairs by the window and glasses and a bottle of clear liquid on a table. Langner reached out, pulled back a chair for Molly and waved her into it as though she was a very fragile and valuable piece of property.

'Please sit down, Mr Easter,' he said. 'I'm afraid this room is rather small, but I reserved it for obvious reasons as a vantage point. We can observe our quarry much better from here than standing amongst *that*.' He pointed down at the crowd and then moved to the table. 'A little schnapps, perhaps. We still have ten minutes to go.'

'Good!' We had nodded and he filled the glasses and handed two of them to us and raised his own. '*Prosit*. To the success of your mission, whatever that may really be.' He raised his glass in a single practised motion and drained it with one gulp, but I sipped mine with more caution.

I like the strong, bitter taste of *Korn*, but know its powers, and I wished to keep my head clear. From where we sat, I could look at the scene below as from a theatre box or a grandstand, and I remembered a similar scene I had witnessed years ago. I can't recall the actual year, but the place was Dartmoor, the month was December or January, and the event was the release of a wife-beater who had served seven years.

Similar, but so different! A cold, grey morning, with drizzle blowing across the heather and into the prison yard. The woman with her daughter standing against a wall to keep out of the wind. The postern opening and a little man coming out and walking shamefacedly forward. The women staring at him for a moment, their faces working, seeming to turn away at first and then rushing towards him with their arms open. Pathetic, sad – maybe tragic, but nothing to do with the sunlit release of Erik Brenner.

'Ten minutes to go and here come the family.' Langner's voice interrupted my memories, and I saw an open Mercedes moving through the crowd, towards the gate. A heavily veiled woman sat in the back with a middle-aged man beside her. 'His wife and his son, Karl,' Langner said. 'Karl was largely responsible for obtaining Papa Erik's release. He wrote to the newspapers. He wrote a book entitled *The Lonely Man at Spandau*. He petitioned the Bundestag and the Allied Governments, and after almost forty years he won. But what will he see after such a long incarceration? A ghost, a senile maniac, a reed broken by the wind, as the Hebrew Bible puts it; a repentant sinner? Well, we shall know soon, and in the meantime, a drop more to drink, perhaps?'

'No, not for me,' Molly answered and I shook my head as Langner raised the bottle again. Something was happening at last.

More troops had mounted the steps and faced the crowd with fixed bayonets. And the crowd were no longer silent. They had raised their heads and had started to sing. '*Deutschland, Deutschland über Alles,*' they sang and, though I've never claimed to be musical, everyone who isn't completely tone-deaf knows the tune of that battle song. The woman in the Mercedes had drawn back her veil and climbed out of the car. Kirk had described Langner as an efficient operator, but his watch was slow. Somewhere in the distance a clock began to strike the hour, and the door was opening. Out through the doorway stepped Erik Brenner.

'Good grief!' I heard myself mutter above the melody of the hymn, and I had every reason to feel surprised. The man hadn't altered. Not in the least. He was over eighty years old, he had spent nearly half of those years behind bars. He was generally regarded as a harmless and somewhat pathetic lunatic, but that view was completely wrong. Papa Erik had put on a little weight, his skin had a slight prison pallor, he'd lost most of his hair, but that was all. His face and expression were the same: arrogant, self-possessed and full of assurance, the same look which had sneered at the judges in Nuremberg.

For perhaps fifteen seconds, though they seemed like minutes, Brenner's pale blue eyes studied the singing crowd, and then he straightened his shoulders, his right arm shot forward in a National Socialist salute and he walked down the steps. He paused to kiss his wife. The uniformed chauffeur let the clutch in and the Mercedes drove off; six motor cyclists followed as an escort.

The celebration was over.

* * *

'No, not a reed shaken by the wind!' I looked at Langner and grimaced. 'Hardly touched by a storm, I'm afraid, so what now? I think you said the party starts in a few minutes.'

'At 4.45 sharp, but I think you should not be too punctual, Herr Easter.' He frowned at his faulty watch and then delved in his pocket and produced a thick envelope. 'Your invitations to the gathering, my friends, but please be careful with them. Cost a lot to borrow an original to forge. Took a lot of skill to produce a copy.

'Yes, a very select gathering. Purely restricted to the Reich-minister's family and his former friends and their relations. Most exclusive, and here is what I have prepared for you.' He pulled out a pocket notebook and squinted at a page. 'My car will drive you to the Hotel Bristol, where rooms have been reserved for you. The Hotel Bristol is only five minutes walk from the Frankreich. You will arrive there at 5.30 and should be introduced to Erik Brenner, though he may not remember your uncle's real name, Mrs Bloom. Refresh his memory with the term: *Operation GNR*.'

'I'm sorry, Mr Langner,' Molly obviously didn't understand the initials, and neither did I, if it came to that. 'GNR. What operation are you talking about?'

'*Gross Gott*, and you said that General Kirk had briefed you!' Langner clicked his teeth to register irritation. 'R stands for Ryde, of course, and the G and N are the first and last letters of the word *Grauen*.

'*Das Grauen*, Fräulein Bloom.' He attempted to explain, but made a hash of it. 'Gruesome might fit. A gruesome, fearful thing. The worst thing in the world, as your George Orwell said. Something too unspeakable to be mentioned, but you must mention those initials to our quarry if you wish him to speak to you.

'Our quarry.' He broke off and then started to quote a line of English verse: 'I met Murder in the way, he had a mask like Castlereagh.' He looked at the crowd slowly dispersing and then at his inaccurate watch. 'Well, let us go. Say ten minutes to the Bristol, twenty minutes to change, and for you to have a shave, Mr Easter.' The blond, bearded bastard glanced at my stubbled chin. 'Five minutes to the Frankreich and say an hour at the outside there. We shall meet back at the Bristol, at 7 o'clock precisely.'

★ ★ ★

The Hotel Frankreich stood at the end of the Königsallee, a long, winding road that runs through the forest they call the Green Wood. The area must have been a kind of millionaires' row before the war, and its former prosperity had returned. There was little sign of the heavy street fighting which had destroyed many of the buildings. The ruins had been demolished or rebuilt, and they ranged from modernistic cubes of glass and concrete to Victorian mansions with towers and spires soaring above the trees. Every type of architectural perversity was displayed in the Grünewald, and in my mind, the district was a sort of plutocratic gipsy encampment. Each house was surrounded by walls or fences topped with barbed wire and seemed to be in a perpetual state of siege.

The Frankreich certainly was, and we were checked at the gate before being allowed to wander through a collection of some of the most magnificent motor cars I had ever seen. We were five minutes later than Hans Langner had anticipated, when we mounted a long Gothic staircase and we were stopped again.

'I am sorry, sir and madam.' Two tall middle-aged men, who in earlier days might have warmed the cockles of Hitler's twitching heart, blocked our way. 'The doorman telephoned to say you were coming, but I have to inform you that we have no accommodation for the general public this evening, and the hotel is closed.'

'Oh dear, do I look like a member of the general public, *Sturmtrooper*?' One of them had spoken in German, Molly replied in the same language, and her question was valid. Molly had changed into a low-cut white dress which no Carthage Road class had knocked up. That dress came from Paris, and she resembled a queen. She also spoke like one and gave me a regal nudge with her elbow. 'Tell the man who we are, Bill, and show him our invitations.'

'Ah, *Herr Easter und Frau Bloom*.' I'd produced our two forged cards, and he squinted at them and then handed them over for his colleague's inspection.

'*Ja, Franz. Alles in ordnung. Entshuldigen Sie mir bitte, gnä'es Frau*.' The colleague was satisfied and he bowed. Number One damn near grovelled.

'A thousand pardons, Mrs Bloom,' he said. 'Do please forgive our stupidity. You see we are under strict orders to admit no unauthorized persons to the Minister's reception, and most of the guests have already arrived.' With deft, almost feminine dexterity, he removed Molly's coat with one hand and clicked the fingers of the other. '*Schnell, Schmidt. Sehr schnell*. The boy will take you up immediately, Mrs Bloom. Your servant, Mr Easter.'

The summons had sent a bent, aged and incredibly tiny figure hurrying like a crab towards us and he clicked his heels and bowed even lower.

'Invoice,' Molly whispered, as we followed the boy upstairs towards the sounds of revelry. 'To Herr Brenner in account with the Hotel Frankreich. To boot-licking of guests, 50 Deutschmark West.'

The reception room was low and long and seemed to have been constructed mainly of glass and stainless steel. Though only about a hundred guests were present, the reflections made them appear like a multitude.

'Good evening, Fräulein, and allow me to introduce myself. My name is Klaus, Count von Wessel.' A man by the door stooped, kissed Molly's hand and made a number of guttural noises which sounded like insults, though he was probably only trying to be pleasant. 'A very good evening for the Reich and the people of this, our country, so what may I ask you to drink?'

'How do you do, Count, but it is Frau, not Fräulein. I am a widow. And this is my friend Herr William Easter,' Molly replied to him in faultless German. 'We are both from London.'

'Mr Easter. How are you, sir?' The Count had a completely vacant face which only a monocle seemed to hold together. 'London; the greatest city in Europe. I know it very well, and your presence here makes the minister's release an international occasion.

'*Herr Ober*,' his hand shot out and arrested a waiter in full flight. 'Now, what are your joint poisons to be? Ah, champagne for Madame, and a Scotch and water for the Herr. No, nothing for me, thank you; I am on duty and have enough minerals to propose a toast.'

The waiter had hurried away and Wessel raised his glass of tonic or soda or whatever it was. 'To the example, fortitude and the long life and happiness of Reichminister Erik Brenner.' I sipped my Scotch, Molly took a drop of champagne, but there was more to come, and the Count continued. 'Also to the basic culture of our brother nations.

'But *natürlich*. I worked for your Control Commission for a time and I understand the situation as our Führer did. Adolf Hitler never wanted to make war against his brothers, and that is why he spared you in 1940. The Luftwaffe could have flattened your cities, the *Unterseebootenmenshaften* could have left you to starve, but they were ordered to hold their hands, but why – why, Mr Easter?'

'I've really no idea, Count,' I said and I almost meant it. I might have mentioned the RAF or the British Navy, spoken about our gallant Merchant Seamen, the boys and girls of the ARP and ATS and a dozen other heroic bands of brothers and sisters, but it was too much trouble. The atmosphere in the room was too thick and the cries of Hunnish merriment too noisy. If Count von Wessel wanted to talk, let him.

'Ach, you yield, Mr Easter. Your friend cannot reply to my enquiries, Frau Bloom, so may I explain about culture?' He proceeded to do so, and though I tried to ignore his lecture, I failed. 'Language to start with. The whole basis of the British tongue is Teutonic. Anglo-Saxon perverted by a slight smattering of Norman French, which of course originates from the Vikings – our fellow explorers.' Whether Erik the Red, or old Ragnar Hairybreeks would have gone along with that, I don't know, but I did know that I was bloody bored with Count von Wessel's *Horst Liebe*. 'Poetry, for example, Mrs Bloom,' he continued. 'The great Chaucer and Shakespeare are known to be of genuine German descent, and if you compare their works with many of our poets, such as Schiller, Goethe and Wagner, you will recognize the connection, Mrs Bloom.'

'Schiller?' Molly frowned at the idiotic creature for a moment, and then her face cleared. 'Ah yes, I have read some Schiller. A wonderful writer, but we call him Shelley, in English.'

'Shelley! How interesting, and I did not know that they were the same person. Proves my point, though, and I must make a note of the names.' He pulled out a diary and a pencil and started to make his note, when we were interrupted.

'Ah, there you are, Klaus.' Frau Brenner was even smaller and older than she had looked at the prison. She had changed into a bright blue costume and used make-up lavishly, but neither could conceal the lines of her face and body. Only her eyes seemed active. They were very bright and intelligent and they stared suspiciously at Molly. 'Please introduce me to your friends. I don't believe we have met before.'

'Of course, Magda.' The Count lowered his diary. 'Allow me to present Miss – sorry, Mrs Bloom and Mr Easter, both great admirers of your husband from England.'

'Then I am delighted to welcome you here, and apologize for my ignorance. How did you come to know my husband, Mrs Bloom?'

'She didn't, Frau Brenner. Neither of us did.' Molly had hesitated; quick thinking was necessary and I stepped into the breach.

'My father, Captain Easter, was a guard at Spandau and he was killed in a motor accident last year.' The real old bastard had shuffled off his mortal coils more than twenty years back, and he'd never been in the army, but little Madam Brenner wasn't to know that, and I expanded the lie. 'He and your husband became very friendly in the prison and he sent Dad an invitation from there. I wrote back about Dad's sad end and mentioned that Mrs Bloom and I are engaged to be married. You can imagine how surprised and delighted I was to receive two personal cards.'

'Congratulations on your nuptials, Herr Easter, and how kind of Erik; how touching.' I didn't know whether she'd swallowed the yarn or not, but it didn't matter. All I had to do was to introduce Molly to the former war criminal. Her next statement suggested we'd get the chance. 'My husband is resting in another room at the moment. Today's events have tired him considerably, but I am sure he will wish to meet the son of an old friend and his wife to be.

'Will you excuse us, please, Klaus,' she asked the Count, but Wessel was eager to come too and said so, with a deal of pathos.

'Oh, very well, but don't tire Erik too much, and leave as soon as I give the word.' Our hostess turned and led the way through the reception room, to a door on the right. She rapped the panel three times and waited till a gruff voice ordered her to enter.

'Erik,' she said, when we were all inside the little private study. 'I am sorry to disturb you, my dear, but I know you would wish to greet the son of an old friend from England and his bride to be.'

'Friend. English friend? Then, let us speak in English, Magda.' Erik Brenner lolled back on a sofa, but he eased himself up and looked at Molly. His expression was rather pleasant and gentle, and his eyes were just the eyes of a tired old man, who had spent a long time in prison. But the mouth . . .

I can't really describe Erik Brenner's mouth, but it was one of the cruellest things I had ever seen on a human being. No lips – just a gash that might have been sliced with a razor across the tight bladder of his face.

'Easter,' he said, after his wife had introduced us. 'No, I have a good memory, but I cannot recall meeting any Captain Easter at Spandau, though there was a Sergeant Lent.

'But you, my dear. Your face is somehow familiar, but I cannot place it.' His eyes glowered at Molly with good humour, but it was just a trick. Behind the eyes I sensed the thing which had made the mouth the terrible shape it was. 'Maybe I knew your family in London, Mrs Bloom. I was attached to our embassy there in 1939.'

'No, Herr Minister, not in '39 and not in London, and I'm afraid we are gatecrashers here.' Molly blurted out the admission before I could stop her. 'You knew my uncle, though. After 1944, you called him Mr GNR.'

And those initials did it. Brenner was on his feet, and they hit him right in the centre of the bullseye. He staggered slightly and gripped the back of the sofa to support himself. His tiny mouth opened and he made me think of a punch-drunk boxer reeling against the ropes. 'Magda,' he said. 'Will you and Count von Wessel leave us for a moment? Wait on the balcony, if you wish, but I must talk to these people alone.

'Thank you, my dear.' He watched them go out through a pair of French windows and then drew the curtains and turned to Molly. 'Now, Mrs Bloom, you claim to be a relative of Ryde's, so can you prove the relationship?'

Without speaking, Molly opened her handbag and passed him an envelope. 'Yes,' he said looking at the contents. 'Two photographs and a letter to your mother, sent her via Spain in 1944. That is Tommy Ryde's handwriting, so I believe you. I am also sorry for you, but how can I help?'

'Don't you understand, Minister? Can't you see what I want – what I need to know? I wasn't even born when Tom defected, but all my life has been haunted by his memory – his ghost.' There was no hint of play-acting in Molly's voice. 'What became of that ghost, Minister? My uncle gave his last broadcast from Hamburg in '44 and then he vanished. What happened to him after that?'

'I see. I see your point quite clearly, but what can I say? It was such a long time ago.' He waved us to a couple of chairs and lit a cigarette. 'Mrs Bloom, all that I can tell you will probably hurt a great deal, but I gather ignorance is even more painful.' He watched Molly nod and pulled at the cigarette. 'Then, let's start at the beginning.

'When I first met Tom Ryde, I was in charge of all exterior radio broadcasts from the Reich to Great Britain, and he came to me on trial, purely as an announcer. And he was good, damned good.' The minister paced the floor, and his cigarette smoke drifted to the ceiling like a trail of the lost years. 'I appointed him scriptwriter and producer after a few months, and the programmes became even better – the most effective propaganda we ever managed to transmit, but too – too effective.

'You see, these things work both ways, Mr Easter. Like poison gas or germ warfare, for example. If one side adopts the technique, the enemy may follow.' He paused and stared down at me. 'Our losses in Russia were mounting, we were being kicked out of Africa, and the Allied air assaults were increasing. We had no desire that the British should follow Ryde's example, and he was told to lower the tone. He agreed, but there was one condition: free access to all POW camps. That was when he got his nickname – when he started to change.'

'To change?' Molly sat rigid in her chair staring up at him. 'How, Minister? What was the change?'

'I do not know, my dear, and I thank God for my ignorance.' He paused for a second and flicked the ash from his cigarette. 'I am a real German, Mrs Bloom. A National Socialist German, and I regret nothing that I did. Nothing at all, because it was done for the Fatherland and Adolf Hitler, our Leader.

'But with your uncle, it was different. I do not believe that he betrayed his country because of political motivation or gain. The end didn't matter a scrap to him, only the means: the interest in pain. No, manipulation and the destruction of a soul are probably better ways to describe it, and – let me think.' He turned and stood with his back against the French windows. 'Yes, I watched him interrogate a young boy once. A British merchant seaman, I believe it was, and your uncle seemed to mesmerize him. Just sat and listened and then talked. It didn't matter what he said, and the words signified nothing. But something else happened, like a wire or a radio wave passing between them, and that young man responded to the signal. After half an hour, he was like putty in Tom Ryde's hand and offered to broadcast for us.

'I don't know what the power was. Something non-physical or supernatural perhaps, but I do know this: I, Erik Brenner, a war criminal from Spandau, feared it.'

And I could see that Molly shared his feelings. I could read her thoughts. The broadcasts were nothing compared to this, she kept telling herself. This was horrible, but even the horror brought hope. Every word of Brenner's was taking her nearer to the truth. The search for Tommy Ryde and what became of him.

'And then, Minister,' she said. 'What happened then?'

'He started to decay, Mrs Bloom. A slow process, like dry rot creeping through timber, but just as dangerous. A moral, intellectual and physical decline, as though Tom Ryde had sold his soul to the devil, and was paying for the transaction.

'Drinking and drugs – women, and men too.' The minister closed his eyes to try to blot out the memory. 'Ryde repeatedly got into fights on the Reperbahn. In one club a waitress stabbed him through the hand with an ice pick, and he was badly injured. We never let him go out without a bodyguard after that – a sort of male nurse for his protection.' Brenner opened his eyes and stared at Molly. 'You want me to go on, Mrs Bloom? Really want it?'

'Very well.' Molly had nodded and he cleared his throat and continued. 'Ryde made his last broadcast in December 1944, and when it was finished, he collapsed in the studio. The doctors found that his body was almost completely paralysed and he was sent to a hospital in Bavaria. Don't know what treatment they gave him there, but he was unconscious in the ambulance and that was almost the last time I saw him.

'Yes, almost the last time. Ten days later I received a personal letter from Himmler. In his own hand and very stiff and formal as always, but the message was clear enough. Your uncle was to be presumed dead. All papers relating to him must be destroyed.

It had become a treasonable offence even to mention the name of Thomas Ryde.

'That is all I can tell you, dear lady. You are the first people with whom I have discussed Ryde since receiving the Reichführer's orders.'

'No, not all, Minister. Almost!' Molly was on her feet and he drew back the curtains. 'You said "Almost the last time I saw him." You repeated those words twice, so tell me what they meant. Where did you see Tom Ryde again?'

'In Norway it was, and quite by chance. We still were in control there, and I went to Bergen to try to get away, but there was no room.' A car backfired in the street and Brenner's thin mouth opened wider. 'No room for me. Dr Loser had taken Ryde to the U . . .' The lips closed and he toppled forward. I'm afraid I never heard the last word. All I heard was the sound of the shot that killed him!

CHAPTER SEVEN

'Brenner dead!' Having been grilled by the German police, interrogated by the German Secret Service, and damn near tortured by a female German doctor, Molly and I were allowed to return home, but we received no welcome there. The boss was not pleased with our progress. The old brute appeared ruddy furious.

'I know the fellow's dead, Billy, but you say he died without speaking to you.' Kirk snorted and kept pounding his desk in irritation. 'No last words – no dying message?'

'Not that I can recall,' I said, but Molly had a better memory. 'I think he mentioned a man and a place,' she said. 'A Dr Loser, a town in Norway, Bergen, and he also used the letter "U" before the bullet caught him.'

'U. That fits – fits like a glove, and I'm glad you went along, my dear.' His eyes twinkled at Molly, and I thought of how Brenner's eyes had looked when he died and how his killer had reacted as I rushed out at him. Count von Wessel was leaning against a balustrade with the revolver pointing at his head, and he smiled before pulling the trigger. *'Kultur, Mein Herr,'* he said. *'Kultur Kampf,* Herr Easter.'

The blast and the third bullet opened his skull, but the gun had been fired before, as Frau Brenner learned to her cost, though the second bullet didn't kill her outright. The *gnädiges Frau* lived for about ten minutes after the police arrived, and she talked to 'em. I didn't hear a word that she said, for obvious reasons. After passing through von Wessel's scalp, the third missile had ricocheted from the wall and struck my left foot. The big toe was still bandaged.

'Stop moaning about your flesh wound, Bill.' I'd either spoken aloud, or Kirk had demonstrated his mind-reading abilities again. 'What's a grazed foot compared to assassination, and Erik Brenner was assassinated, not just murdered. He was liquidated, to stop him talking, and the last thing he mentioned was the letter "U", Molly Bloom.

'"U" for U-boat, my dear, and I'm not shooting a line. I know.' He gobbled at Molly, like an outraged gander. 'I've got friends everywhere you see, and some of them work for the West German Intelligence Corps; and they all have telephones. I spoke to my pals after hearing of our Billy's trivial accident, and I learned a great deal from them. Almost enough to say that Tommy Ryde is still alive and kicking.

'No, I'm not sure where he is, Bill.' He shrugged at my question. 'If I was sure, I wouldn't be sitting here wasting time with you, so I'll give you my reasons.

'Your uncle, my dear, was a man with an almost hypnotic personality. His broadcasts and manipulations of prisoners in the camps prove that.' He paused, dragged at his cigar and blew an almost perfect smoke ring that circled Molly's head like a halo. 'But as Brenner informed you and Bill, Ryde went batty. Took drugs, as well as booze to excess. Got into street fights and bar brawls in Hamburg and other places. Behaved so badly that Himmler ordered medical treatment for the Nazis' unreliable ally.' Another drag, and another smoke ring. 'Ryde was sent to a hospital on the Bodensee in southern Germany and placed in the hands of a certain Dr Joel Loser. What treatment Ryde received, we can't say, but we do know that during April 1945, at almost the very end of the war, he was taken to Bergen and shipped out on a U-boat.

'Maybe to South America, Bill. A possible destination, but unlikely, if you use your imagination and think logically.' He discarded my suggestion with a wave of his Corona. 'By 1945, only the insane imagined Germany could win the war by conventional weapons, but the Nazis were not sane, and their creed was based on Nihilism: destruction of society for its own sake.

'Don't talk to me about the Thousand Year Reich, woman.' He had rounded on Molly for just mentioning the term. 'That was just a pipe-dream, a rallying cry, and Hitler never intended to found any such thing. His aim was to wipe out Germany, the whole world, and the bastard almost succeeded.

'Yes, Adolf Hitler was mad, Bill, and several of his intimate followers shared the same complaint. They refused to accept defeat at any cost, and even today a handful may still be fighting on.

'With what, you may ask.' He frowned at me, though I hadn't said a word for some time, and continued the discourse . . . 'Your leader is dead, your troops are exhausted, so how would you carry out your bent crusade, Bill? Remember that the aims are destruction, disruption and total annihilation. What forces can you still employ?

'Mercenaries, my boy?' Kirk appeared amused by my answer. 'You haven't got any money to pay the blighters with. No, hired killers are out, and they only exist in cheap works of fiction and your own puerile imagination. Give the villain a few hundred quid and he may stab a stranger in a dark street, but we're not talking about strangers. We're discussing the big lads. All the major allied leaders had to be wiped out. Churchill, Roosevelt, Stalin – the lot. Hired assassins wish to survive and enjoy their pay, after the job's completed. They won't risk their own lives and face certain death.'

'Assassins, General,' Molly pronounced the word strangely. 'The Hashishim. Abah Sabah – the Old Man of the Mountains.'

'Warmer, my dear. A little warmer, but not right in the fire yet.' Kirk nodded at her. 'Kamikaze fanatics do exist, as we know to our cost, but they are usually drawn from the eastern races: Arabs, Japanese and such like.' He stressed the racial inferiority.

'Sabah fed his followers hashish, as a taste of paradise to come, and they knocked off a lot of enemies, but that was a long time ago, and we're talking about Europeans, who are far less gullible.

'Charlotte Corday, Princips at Sarajevo, Vlada Georgiev who murdered the King of Yugoslavia, and the blighter who bumped off Lincoln. Where would you find such paragons today, Bill and Molly?

'Right at last, children: in a bin.' I'd settled for mental home, Molly had mentioned asylum, but naturally old Kirk preferred a vulgar, slang term. 'A bin on the Bodensee. A nut-house run by Dr Joel Loser, may hell keep hot for him.' He took a last pull at his cigar and stubbed out the butt.

'My contacts in Germany couldn't say exactly when Dr Loser started his chamber of horrors, because the place was bombed by the RAF in 1945, and the records all went for a Burton. Most of the staff and inmates went the same way, but Ryde and Loser weren't amongst them. You told us what Brenner said, Molly. They were in Bergen, joining a Nazi submarine, long after the holocaust. A pity that Erik Brenner didn't manage to give you the boat's number and destination before he died, but I've got the First Sea Lord's Office working on that problem.' He put on his spectacles and opened an exercise book; the kind of thing school children are given, with useful information about the metric system printed on the covers, and a list of 'Danger Don'ts'.

'Now, I've jotted down what we do know for sure, and I'll read the notes aloud for you – condensing as far as possible.'

He proceeded to do so, but he didn't 'condense'. To me, the verb means 'to compress', 'to grow dense', 'to make shorter', but apparently Kirk used a different dictionary. He read the notes out in full, slowly, pedantically, and my head reeled. I won't bore you with his actual words but attempt a synopsis.

In 1944 Dr Joel Loser was put in charge of a mental institution not far from the Swiss border. A number of psychopaths were provided for him as experimental subjects, and his experiments proceeded. Kirk was pretty vague about what the methods were, but obviously the end seemed clear: to produce manic killers, who would commit murder with no thought of the consequences.

I suppose the word 'fanatic' is the only one that really fits, though not political fanaticism. Oh no, politics were small beer, and Dr Joel started with religion.

Take a pious loonie and encourage his beliefs. Pander to his fears and give them faces. In time, the Devil will arise, in many forms: Eisenhower disguised as Satan, Voroshilov looking remarkably like the Prince of Darkness, Montgomery with the pan of Beelzebub. All big and remarkably evil pots, who had to be dealt with and struck down in the cause of righteousness.

Kirk didn't know what Ryde's role in the establishment really was, as a patient or an assistant. But he was said to be suffering from paralysis of the nervous system, and certain treatment was meted out to him. Probably a form of ECT, though no one was sure about that.

What was certain is that the holy war was due to start, when Kirk's brave boys got wind of the doctor's intentions and the RAF flew in. Thirty tons of high explosives were blasted on the hospital, and there were only two known survivors. The good doctor and Tommy Ryde, who turned up later in Bergen.

'Fair enough, Molly? Penny dropped, Bill?' Kirk had completed his monologue and waited for comments. I was about to say that several hundred pence had clattered down, but I didn't get the chance. The phone was ringing and the ancient warrior reached out to answer it. 'General Kirk here,' he replied. 'Ah, yes, of course, I would like to talk with him.

'Scotland Yard, Bill,' he muttered to me. 'The Commissioner, in person. Told the feller to keep in touch, in case you-know-what happens.

'Good day to you, Sir Stanley,' he said jovially, when his contact came through. 'How nice to hear from you, dear boy. Keeping well, I hope. No recurrence of that damned back business? Horrible things, slipped discs.

'What? In Southford again? Repeat that very slowly, please, and I'll jot it down.' He lifted his ballpoint and held it over a sheet of paper.

'Slower, Sir Stanley, and stop gibbering. I want the facts, not a series of gasps and stutters. Yes, that's better – a little better.' His hand travelled quickly across the page, and then he threw the pen aside.

'Now, listen to me, Commissioner. I want those two men, and I want 'em alive and kickin'. I know they're armed. I know they've killed at least three people, but that's neither here nor there. They must be captured intact, and I've been expecting something of the kind.' The other voice rumbled in protest, but Kirk brushed it aside. 'Three means nothing, and I'm not talking about coincidences; these crimes tie up with the others and they might – might just lead us to friend Ryde.

'Goodbye, for the moment, Sir Stanley, and I'll be down at Southford within an hour or so and take over there. And no shooting and no gas either. Keep those blighters *compos mentis* and in good health, because if they're not – if any one of them is harmed in any way, we'll be in trouble.' He banged down the instrument and looked at me. 'Yes, real trouble, Billy Easter!'

CHAPTER EIGHT

'Carter and Wolfe.' I was driving the car, Kirk was in the back seat with Molly, and he kept leaning over my shoulder and repeating the words. 'Don't forget the men's names, and don't forget what I've told you about them either. They mustn't be killed. I want 'em both alive and kicking.'

'*Zu befiel, Herr Kirk – ich verstehe, mein Gruppenführer.*' I don't know why I answered in German, but probably weariness and pure frustration had a lot to do with it. I'd been grilled by the Krauts for hours in Berlin. I'd been hunched over the steering wheel for almost an hour, while Kirk had been busy with a radio set, delivering the news and issuing instructions.

'Stop dawdling, man. Get your foot on the accelerator and keep it there. Look out, you bloody fool. Didn't you see that those traffic lights were red?'

Less speed – more haste was clearly the order of the day, and the old brute's vehicle was a right bitch to handle. A supercharged Mercedes staff car, which would have looked well in a museum, but was the pride and joy of its owner, who had acquired it after *der Dritte Reich's* collapse. He called the beast Betty, and she'd first seen the light of day around 1940. She weighed more than two tons but had no power steering. The supercharger gave her a fair turn of speed, but there were no springs to speak of. No proper brakes either, though a lot of roundabouts lay on the road to Southford. My foot ached with pushing the bloody pedal.

A right bitch, as I've remarked, a horrible journey, but it was almost ending, and we would soon be there. I turned off the supercharger and tried to remember Kirk's news summary.

Carter and Wolfe. Two young lunatics, who had been transferred to the care of the county mental hospital, ten miles from Southford, though the care hadn't lasted long; after twenty-three hours, to be exact, Messrs C & W decided to make off. They had killed and robbed a male nurse and a resident psychiatrist. They had driven to Southford in the psychiatrist's car. They had broken into a sports goods shop and acquired a couple of shotguns and an adequate supply of ammunition. They had turned their guns on an oversuspicious policeman who was not expected to survive his wounds. They were now holed up in a partially demolished slum area down by the docks. What business they were of ours, I didn't know, but we were soon to find out, and Kirk's voice rasped in my ear.

'Turn right at the next junction, Billy, and then take the second on the left. Yes, we are here.'

I stopped the car and looked around for a moment. As I've told you, the area was described as a partially demolished slum, and the description was correct. Half the houses had been torn down already, and the rest stood empty and forlorn waiting for the bulldozers. Forlorn and also indecent, in the glare of the searchlights. Elderly, sagging striptease artists on a fairground stage. To the right lay a railway embankment, to the left was the river; behind, a wasteland of dispirited grass and rubble sloped down to the sea.

'Ah, it's you, General Kirk.' A police inspector pointed a torch in the car. 'Glad you made it, but I'm afraid you're just in time for the kill. I don't believe you've met Dr Grace and Dr Rowe, yet?'

'No, but Mr Easter has.' Kirk climbed out and bowed to Helen Grace, who wore a raincoat and fur-lined boots and looked as brisk and efficient as usual. 'A bad business, madam, though I didn't realize that Carter and Wolfe were patients of yours.'

'They were till recently, General.' She acknowledged my presence with a brief nod, and gave Molly a friendly smile. 'Jimmy Carter and Paul Wolfe suffered from dementia praecox and came to us as private patients a year ago, but the condition worsened, though don't ask me why. They both became violent and had to be transferred to public health for safety reasons.' She turned to Rowe, who was tall and thin and spoke with a stammer.

'I never met either of the two, General Kirk,' he said. 'And Dr Wilson, the psychiatrist in charge of them, is dead. Poor man –

a dedicated, good man, John Wilson. Really fond of his patients, and regarded them as distressed children. How could he have gone wrong in giving that couple insulin, General Kirk?'

'An unfair question to put to a layman, Dr Rowe.' A cold wind was blowing and Kirk tightened up his jacket. 'I know that insulin is a substance that eats up sugar in the blood stream, but that is about all that I really do know.'

'And you're right, General. Sugar produces energy, so we give insulin to drive it out. The idea is to create a vacuum, and leave the brain torpid and lifeless for a period. To give a patient a chance to dry out.'

'And that couple were in the process of drying out, as you put it, Dr Rowe.'

'They should have been, General, but something went wrong – terribly wrong.' Rowe's stammer increased. 'The idea is to strip the brain of its abnormal fancies and allow it to adjust to normality. To build an emptiness ready for self-expression and sanity, though that didn't happen.' Rowe slurred the words as though he was drunk. 'The coma lasts for approximately forty-five minutes at the outside. Carter and Wolfe were about to approach the coma stage when something happened.

'No, I do not know what it was.' He frowned at Kirk's question. 'The minds should have been blank, the bodies terribly weak, but they weren't. It was almost as if the men were possessed and taken over by another, alien personality. I know that doesn't make sense, but it's all I can think of.'

'It makes very good sense if you consider the past, Dr Rowe.' Kirk turned to Grace. 'But tell me, Doctor. What would happen if the patient came round now?'

'Death, General Kirk.' Grace spoke with complete confidence. 'Yes, they would die all right and I don't know what's keeping them alive now. Those two boys have been deprived of sugar for over four hours. Their bodies must have dried up, and during the treatment one has to be very careful and watch every symptom. After the crisis has been reached, neat glucose must be injected at once. I have two syringes here, but . . .'

'But no, madam.' The police inspector interrupted her. 'Nobody is going to approach those two maniacs till they're fast asleep. Till the gas cylinders are delivered in fact.

'Riot gas, General. That's the only way to stop them, and I've asked Aldershot to send us a consignment and a trench mortar. The lorry should be here at any moment, and then the matter ends.'

'Riot gas, Inspector.' Kirk frowned at him. 'Isn't that a bit risky, after what Dr Grace has just told us?'

'Risky, you say. Got a better solution?' The inspector returned Kirk's frown. 'Those chaps have killed three men already, and they're not murdering any more. I'll accept full responsibility for anything that happens, and there's the truck now.' He turned and pointed at a heavy lorry emerging through a bridge under the embankment. Three soldiers sat in the front seat, and more were clustered behind. 'Yes, that's her, and in ten minutes we can start shooting.'

'Ten minutes, you say. Then give me your syringes, please, Dr Grace.' Kirk held out his hand and took the package from her. 'Thank you, and I'll be on my way.' Without another word he stuffed the box into his pocket and strode forward.

And Molly followed him; that was the crazy thing. I would have let the old brute face the storm of gunshot pellets alone and wished him the best of British luck, but that stupid little cow tripped off after him through the gloom.

I stood there watching them, and waiting to see Kirk stagger and fall down as the shots caught him. Waiting to hear Molly scream. Odd that they didn't appear to get any further away. And why were my own feet moving? I had no desire to share Kirk's fiery end. I had nothing to do with the two armed maniacs. I just hoped to stay with the police, and watch the show in comfort and safety. If Molly wanted to play heroine to Kirk's Sir Galahad, let her – no business of mine. 'Let the dead bury their dead' is a sound proverb. Not my affair, so why was I following the old bastard? Why was I striding across the rubble with the searchlights lighting me up as a clear target, an offering for suicide?

'Ah, there you are, Bill.' Kirk grinned as I came abreast of them. 'Good show – better late than never, as usual, but here goes.' A shot rang out wiping the smug smile from his face, but he didn't slow down, though a blast of pellets whistled past us. He opened his mouth and gripped Molly's left arm. To my astonishment, he started to sing.

'I'm a broken hearted keelman and I've long been in love
With a young lass from Gateshead and I call her me dove.'

I think the song was some kind of Geordie ballad, but I only remember a few words. Over the embankment a train was pulling out and heading north, on the river a ship's whistle hooted, from the building came another louder report. Only about a hundred yards to go, but none of these things deterred Charlie Kirk. He still brayed the verse tonelessly and with feeling.

'She's a big lass and a bonny lass and she likes her beer,
And they call her Cushie Butterfield and I wish she was here.'

'Come on, Billy. No loitering. Mustn't show the chaps that we're scared of a couple of pop guns.' His normal voice returned, but I wasn't scared and I wasn't frightened. I was bloody terrified of those maniacs, and terror and fear are very different things.

'Dr Grace said that they'll die without glucose, and we mustn't let that happen, must we?' The old voice prattled on, the footsteps strolled forward; and every step was a step towards Calvary. For me that was, though apparently not for Kirk or Molly. She remarked that the wind was getting chilly, he tapped his pocket to see that the syringes were still there, I just shivered and forced my feet to keep moving forward.

Forward towards the house which looked gigantic in the moonlight. Though the roof had gone, the walls and chimneys reared up like towers and battlements, and in a lower room two triple murderers were waiting to welcome us.

'If the blighters are going to fire again, they'll fire soon, because we're well in range of a twelve-bore now. Less than fifty yards to go, so take it easy.' Kirk paused and flicked the ash from his cigar. 'Saunter along, as though you haven't a care in the world, Bill. Keep close beside me, Molly.' Fifty yards, forty, thirty. We were almost there, and only God knows what kept me going. The front door was ajar and I watched Kirk toss aside his cigar and pull it open. The bottom dragging on the floor, the sagging hinges creaking. I followed him and Molly down a short flight of steps, and saw him take a torch out of his jacket. The beam shone into a little room that smelled of dust and wood rot and rubble; also of antiseptic. It was the boys who smelled of that, though I had no time to recognize the odour. One lay on the floor with a gun at his side, and he was obviously dead. The gun had blown half his head off.

But the second boy was not dead. He stood or rather leaned against a wall by the window with the twelve-bore in his hands. He turned and looked at Kirk, and the barrel came up very slowly. Not as though he was holding it at all, but as if the metal itself was rising and dragging his arms with it. He had a pale, freckled face and no expression whatsoever.

'Hullo, son,' Kirk said. 'I dunno who you are, Mr Carter or Mr Wolfe, but to hell with formal introductions. I'm Uncle Charlie and you can put that thing down now. The party's over and it's time to go home.' He strolled forward and his heavy, tired face looked full of compassion. Uncle Charlie – the eternal Dad!

'Oh no, son, you don't want to hurt me.' I saw the trigger finger begin to apply first pressure, but Kirk's maimed hand turned the muzzle aside and then he reached for the syringes in his pocket. 'I'll give you a fix in a moment, but wake up first and tell me about it. Just why did you kill the doctor? Any motivation you can think of?'

'Dr Wilson had . . .' The boy struggled with the gigantic effort of concentration. 'Dr John Wilson had . . .'

'What, laddie?' Kirk prompted him. 'Tell me what the doctor had.'

'He had – had.' The eyes widened and then closed. The voice was barely audible. 'Dr Wilson had ginger hair.'

The whole body sagged and crumpled towards his companion on the floor. 'Bloody hell, the bastard's dead. Insulin killed him, and we were too late,' muttered Uncle Charlie . . . Major General Charles Kirk.

CHAPTER NINE

The maniacs were no more, and the next morning dawned. Under orders as always, Molly and I were dispatched to the Ministry of Defence for further information. We didn't get any at first, and Rear Admiral the Honourable Sir Hugo Treecher didn't merely pace his office floor – he clanked. Like a traction engine, he came, though I suppose one shouldn't blame him for that.

Not Treecher's fault that his left ankle had been severed by a depth charge released during a NATO exercise in the Atlantic. The replacement foot was metal. A bit careless to have left the limb in the charge's path, but hardly contemptible. Rather an inefficient one, you might say, though not an actual stigma. The contemptible things about Sir Hugo were his attitudes, and I'll list them in order of severity. Against myself, against Molly, finally against his assistant, though that wasn't important. Hugo's assistant was a pitiful little Lieutenant Commander named Ricks, who had informed us with pride that he was the commodore of a yacht club near Brighton while we were awaiting admission to the presence.

'Well, Mr Easter, I am at your complete disposal, whatever that means.' Treecher made every syllable vaguely insulting. 'I have been ordered to pass over certain files for your inspection, so which do you want?'

'It wasn't a personal request, sir, but came from my superior, Major General Charles Kirk.'

'Kirk eh? A general officer too! Risen to quite a decent rank in his disreputable profession, and it's a pity he didn't learn a few manners to go with it. But no, sir. He or you asked for those files on the telephone. Ricks gave a perfectly proper reply for once, stating that they would be checked by the Department of Naval Intelligence and the details might be passed on in due course. In return, I get this.' He held out an embossed sheet of paper as though it was a repulsive and germ-ridden object. 'Well, I'm in your hands now, and this orders me to cooperate with you and Mrs Bloom to the fullest extent. I obey orders, but I still think it's uncommonly uncivil. Telling tales out of school. Running behind my back to the First Sea Lord. Why couldn't this feller Kirk come to me in person and have a yarn about the problem? Tell me what the trouble is, instead of sending a couple of subordinates to harass me.'

'We're sorry, Admiral Treecher.' Molly did sound slightly apologetic towards the injured Neptune. 'The fact is that Kirk is a very old man, and time is important.'

'Time – important!' Treecher snorted. 'In the First Lord's Office! Extraordinary thing, but as you are here, we might as well get down to business. Ricks!'

'Sir.' Ricks leapt to attention and raised his voice slightly. 'What is it, Admiral?'

'Don't shout at me like that, Lieutenant Commander. Get those papers sorted out.' Treecher rubbed the side of his purple face and scowled. 'Bawlin' in me ear, like a damned coxswain. Nobody has any manners these days. Learnt yours in that bloody yacht club, I suppose!' He turned a malignant eye on me. 'Do you sail Mr Easter?'

'No, sir, I'm afraid not. Not for sport, that is.'

'Afraid? No need to be afraid. One slight thing in your favour. Gangs of grown men mucking about on sour canals. Callin' themselves by Naval ranks they're not entitled to. Common chaps, as well, some of 'em. Shopkeepers, estate agents, that class of feller. Women as well, footling about half nude. Makes me sick.' He turned like a blight on the unfortunate Ricks. 'Well, don't stand all day jawin' about your miserable hobby, man. I want that information, at the double.'

'At once, sir.' Ricks carried a chart and a pile of foolscap to the desk. 'File BF. Should be all here, Admiral.'

'It had better be, for your sake, man.' Treecher lowered himself onto a chair and then looked up at me. 'But your name rings a bell. Easter: any connection with Captain Easter – old Elephant Easter?'

'Yes, sir.' In far-off memory, I recalled an enormous, ill-tempered relative who also lacked a leg and might easily have answered to 'Elephant'. 'My father's brother – an uncle, sir.'

'Well, well. You don't say. Should have told me before. Saved a lot of bad feeling.' Treecher's face relaxed slightly. 'Wonderful chap, was the Elephant. Ever told you how he crushed his leg?'

'Yes, Admiral.' He had done, in great, heroic detail, and I started to repeat the tale of derring-do. 'My uncle was on a destroyer in '44. The action took place off the North Cape, and the opponent was a ruddy great Hun pocket battleship . . .'

'North Cape – destroyer – pocket battleship!' Treecher soon cut me short. 'Elephant has had you on, Easter. He fell into a dock at North Shields. Crooked his leg against the side of a ship when he was as tight as buggery.

'Oh, I do apologize, Mrs Bloom. A most unfortunate expression, and this won't do.' He donned a pair of spectacles and rummaged through the papers. 'You want to know about a Nazi submarine which left Bergen in April 1945. You heard about her from German sources, but you can't, or won't tell me why she's important. I can do better, however. I know where she is.' Like a showman producing a rabbit, he picked up a roll of film and handed it to me.

I saw that the pictures were very dark and indistinct. There were mountains in the background and a hint of mist in the air. In the centre of one shot, a rock reared out of the water; a rock which moved. I saw it moving, as I flicked through the reel. A cloud of spray covered it, and then the point rose up slowly and then came down. No longer a rock, but a long cigar, sliding under the sea.

'Yes, that's her, Easter. That's the joker, Mrs Bloom. Very poor photography, I'm afraid, but we never managed to tear a strip off the poor bastard who was responsible. Didn't find the reel for weeks after it was taken. Came from the wreckage of a Coastal Command Catalina that had been returning to her base near Loch Ewe, after an Iceland convoy patrol. All very routine, but the boys never got back. Found 'em on top of a mountain called, rather inappropriately, Ben Friendship. The crew had all been killed in the crash, but the plane had obviously been in action. All bombs gone and the fuselage riddled with cannon shells. The only interesting thing was that roll of film.'

'And you think that this . . .' I pointed at the moving rock, 'maybe was the U-boat we're after.'

'Don't be impertinent, Easter. I don't merely think. I wouldn't be wasting your time by guesswork. I am quite certain. And have a squint at this.'

Exhibit 2 was a single photograph and much larger than the others. It appeared to show drawings of a submarine, but the details were almost meaningless to me.

'Yes, that's her. An A10 and one of the last coastal types they completed towards the end of the war. Very small displacement and short range; only speed to recommend 'em really, and armed with the same version of the Oerlikon cannon that fired shells found in the Catalina.

'Now this is the point.' He took up another sheet of paper. 'The boat in the reel shot by the Catalina was of the same type. The step of the bows is quite unique, and only six of them were ever launched. Two were scuttled at Brest, three were captured by the Russians in the Baltic, and that leaves one.' He unrolled the chart and picked up a red pencil. 'One that is lying somewhere around here.' The map showed the north-west corner of Scotland, and he drew a thick line stretching from Durness to Loch Broom. 'Can't get any closer than that, I'm afraid. Not at the moment, though I've got a chap working on the evidence right now. We do know, however, that the Cat' made a definite kill, before crashing, with her belly riddled with shell fragments.

'But what was the U-boat doing so close inshore, Easter? The photographs show that she was less than a mile from the mainland, so can either of you provide an explanation, Mrs Bloom?'

'Could she have been dropping something, Admiral?' Molly peered over the chart. 'An ideal place for it if the sea was calm. Rocky bays, a minor road within walking distance and foggy weather. They'd probably just finished the job when the Catalina spotted them.'

'Dropping what, woman?' Treecher made a noise which might

have been a groan or a belch or a cry of indignation. 'If you're thinking of mines, forget 'em. The A10 class were too small to be fitted as minelayers.'

'No, not mines, sir,' I said. 'Mrs Bloom is thinking of something that had to be taken ashore. Maybe something human . . .' I broke off, because the 'phone had rung at Treecher's elbow and he picked it up hurriedly.

'The Rear Admiral speaking,' he said. 'Oh, it's you, at last, Duncan. About bloody time too. Have you got the location yet?' He grabbed the map from me and lifted his pencil. 'Spey Inlet – half a mile from Loch Broom – ten miles from Ben Friendship.'

'Good, Duncan – very good, though I wasn't far out meself.' He pencilled a cross on the chart and banged down the receiver. 'She's there, Easter. Right there, or what's left of her, which won't be much. The U 1001 sailed from Grimstad Fjord near Bergen in April '45, and she ended up about here with a bomb through her bows. Had a copy of the reel blown up, and Duncan McAlistar recognized the coastline.'

'That help you at all?'

'Yes, Admiral, but we need more. A lot more and this is just the beginning.' I glanced at the First Lord's orders and plucked up courage. 'General Kirk is hoping that you can get her up for us. You see, we need the U-boat's log and her captain's orders.' I waited for the coming outburst, but I was wrong. It never came. Treecher opened his mouth to protest, and then changed his mind. Maybe the enormous, peg-legged ghost of old Elephant Easter had given his blessing to the enterprise. Instead of rage, I was subjected to a long and depressing discourse on ocean salvage.

I learned of wrecks breaking up under pressure, and tides scouring debris over them. Of the inability of divers to work in long stretches; of the deep shelving of the Scottish coast.

'Good grief, man, she's been under water for over thirty years and we can't be sure where the bombs caught her. There's probably not a bulkhead left standing, and twenty feet of shale above the wreckage by now. Only one thing in your favour, really. As far as I know, the Jerries always kept their papers in watertight safes.

If there is one secured, we might have a chance, but have you any idea what the job will cost?'

'No, sir, I'm afraid not.'

'Neither have I, and I can't say that I care.' Treecher suddenly roared with laughter. 'Don't give a damn and it'll do those Scapa chaps good to have a bit of exercise. Right, we'll see about getting the safe up for you.' He studied the cross on the map and then snapped at his assistant. 'Ricks, how clean is your bottom?'

'I beg your pardon, Admiral.' The Lieutenant Commander blushed deeply. 'Not sure exactly what you mean, sir.'

'The sea bottom, you imbecile. What is the geological structure – of the ocean bed – at the position I have indicated – on this chart, Lieutenant Commander?'

'I'll find out, sir.' At each pause, Treecher's hand had thumped the desk, and Ricks bounded over to a bookcase. 'Here we are, sir. Granite, volcanic ash and a little white sand.'

'Good, she shouldn't be silted over, then. And the depth should be around twenty fathoms, I imagine.'

'No, sir, I'm afraid not.' Ricks spoke from behind the book. 'It seems there's a fault, a long valley. It hasn't been accurately sounded but is estimated to be between forty and sixty fathoms in depth. The locals call it the Mouth of Canna.'

'Thank you, my friend. As always, a bringer of cheerful tidings. Sixty, eh?' Treecher made a note on the corner of his map. 'That means twenty-five minute spells and the weather's pretty good, now. But, given just a few big Western Ocean rollers and we'll have had it. Well, what have we got for the job at Scapa, Ricks?'

'Nothing very suitable, I'm afraid, sir.' Ricks turned the pages of a second book. 'But *Gruesome*, Captain Hawes, is on the Clyde carrying out trials. Just been refitted though and has a fresh, untried crew, so . . .'

'Then we'll have to freshen the lads up a bit,' Treecher snorted. 'And give Harlot Hawes a bit of experience. Send a signal to *Gruesome* saying they are to proceed with operations as soon as possible, and book us a couple of sleepers on the night train to Scotland.'

'Tonight, sir. But I was hoping – that is, I thought.' Ricks looked close to tears. 'I think I mentioned that it's our Annual Regatta on Saturday and . . .'

'And therefore, Commander, the fleet must put to sea without its beloved leader. Tonight, Ricks.'

'Yes, sir, of course, sir, but there's one small point, Admiral. That signal to *Gruesome*: it's customary to give code names.'

'Thank you, and what shall the name be?' Treecher stood up and then he glanced with loathing at the First Lord's letter. 'Yes, we shall call the operation *Pressgang*.'

* * *

'So, the Admiral is on his way, my friends. Off to Bonnie Scotland on the night mail, and the best of British luck to him. You and Molly had better join him in a day or two, but we can give this *Gruesome* and her matelots a chance to get started first.' Kirk appeared neither pleased nor excited by our news. He sat in his club with an evening paper at the side of the chair, and his face was quite expressionless. 'Now, tell me, Bill. What do you think about this?' He tossed the *Evening Globe* towards me and smiled – a sort of smile without any trace of warmth or humour.

'WHY? WHAT?' The headlines consisted of just two words, and below them the reporters had really gone to town. 'Verbatim Statement made in the Office of this Newspaper by Mrs Jane Roberts of No 1a Bridecastle, London SE28, in the presence of three witnesses.

' "I don't know why I've come to you, gentlemen. Should have gone to the police, I suppose, but talking to you seemed easier." Mrs Roberts paused to take a sip of tea. "Me husband has always been good to me and we've been married for well nigh twenty years; that's why it's hard to say what happened.

' "My Fred's a postman, and he usually gets home about noon or a little after that. It was 12.30 when I heard him come in, and I was in the kitchen gettin' a meal ready.

' "No, that's wrong, gentlemen. I was just sittin' at the table, and listenin' to the voices. Strange, they sounded; more like echoes than a person speakin' – and the hands." Another pause, and another drink of tea. "One of them had a scar as though something had been pushed through the palm, a long time ago.

'"That's right, sir. A stigmata, like Jesus Christ had, and the voices were like Christ's too. Hypnotic, you could say, and they told me what I must do. What I had to do.

'"Odd it was. Maybe I was imagining things, but I didn't recognize our Fred when the kitchen door opened and he came in. A different smell, different . . .

'"Yes, aura, sir. That's the right word. A stranger tried to kiss me, and I didn't realize it was old Fred, God help me." Mrs Roberts opened her handbag and fumbled inside. "Not till I'd struck him – with this."

'At this moment, Mrs Jane Roberts took a sharpened steak knife out of the bag and cut her throat,' stated the *Globe*. 'She died almost immediately.'

'There's another news flash at the side of the page, Bill and Molly.' Kirk pointed to the item: 'Man stabbed to death in Bridecastle Rd, SE28. Name: Fred Roberts. Weapon used: a steak knife.'

'Well, Molly my dear, that suggests to me that Uncle Tom is alive; very much alive – and kicking.'

CHAPTER TEN

The few days passed and I had to travel alone to Scotland, worse luck, as Molly was otherwise engaged. A miserable journey, by train to Glasgow, bus to Oban, and a Naval car to points north. On the last lap the driver told me that, although the Rannock Moor Arms was small and isolated, Admiral Treecher had managed to make himself pretty comfortable. The driver was right.

'Ah, there you are, Easter,' my host remarked as I stepped out of the conveyance. 'Foul trip, I expect, foul place here, foul climate and foul inhabitants.' Treecher stared with fury at the rock-strewn coastline, the grey Atlantic swell and the gaunt housekeeper, who was lifting my bag out. 'Take that up to Mr Easter's room at once, Mrs MacDawlish, while we have a drink.'

'Aye, of course, sir.' She looked at Treecher and then at me. 'Ah, afraid it's a very wee room, Mr Easter, and you'll have to share it with the Commander. One of the servants' rooms, really, but you see, Admiral Treecher has commandeered all the guest quarters and . . .'

'Nonsense, woman. An exceedingly pleasant little room apart from Ricks, with a good view of the chapel. Would have liked it to meself, if I hadn't needed to be near – near me office.

'Well, don't stand there in this drizzle, Easter. Come on inside, sign the book and we'll have a dram together. That's about the only thing to be said for this dump – they've got some quite drinkable Skye whisky.' He stomped up the stairs into a gloomy hall, grumbling as he went. 'Been stuck in this hellhole for half a week already and that's just about enough. Better than living on *Gruesome*, I suppose. A frigate rigged for salvage is no place for a Christian, though Ricks would probably enjoy it. Remind him of his beastly yacht club, I shouldn't wonder. Still, it's tonight or never, praise da Lawd. One way or another, we pack up in a few hours.'

'Tonight, sir?' I asked. 'We got your telephone message, but I couldn't understand the urgency.'

'Didn't you? Thought it was clear enough. I'll explain why, after we've had a drink, but sign the book, man. The aborigines are a very law-abiding lot, and you won't get one without a signature.

'Here, what's that you've written?' He scowled at the damp register and craned over my shoulder. 'W.C. Easter, London. British.

'Were you born up here, or in Wales or Ireland?'

'No, I was born in London, Admiral.'

'London! London is the capital of England, so cross out the British and enter English. No need to imply that you're connected with one of the three degenerate and enslaved races.

'Good. That's better.' I made the alteration and he stomped into a gloomy room, labelled the *Snug*, and bellowed at an aged crone behind the bar. 'Tessie, service please. Two double Skyes and quick about them.

'Well, cheers, Easter.' He looked with love at the two glasses of clear liquid she had placed on the table and lifted his own. 'Now, you were saying that you and General Kirk couldn't understand my signal, though I thought it seemed clear enough.' He emptied his glass and ordered a refill. 'Unless that incompetent fool Ricks made a balls of the text, naturally.'

'Incontinent, Admiral Treecher?' I had raised my glass but lowered it at once. The thought of sharing a room with a man suffering from what I thought he had said, was revolting.

'Not incontinent, Easter. As far as I know, though, he easily could be. But pay attention to what I am about to say to you.' He took a second drink and sat down, jamming his gammy leg against the chair. 'Ricks snores and talks in his sleep, usually about his wretched yacht club, but that's neither here nor there. The point is this.' He scowled towards the window and I saw that the sky was darkening and the sea flecked with foam.

'Yes, looks cheerful, don't it, and before the night's out we'll be in for a ruddy great storm that could pile *Gruesome* up on the rocks. Don't usually trust the Met boys, but today I can smell it.'

He sniffed the atmosphere of peat smoke, beer, stale spirits and tobacco, and produced an old blackened pipe. '*Gruesome*'s heading back to the Clyde as soon as the weather breaks, and it's tonight or never, as far as this month's concerned.'

'And the chances of getting the papers up tonight, Admiral Treecher?'

'Can't honestly say, me boy.' He rammed shag into his pipe, while he spoke. 'Done pretty well so far. Found the wreck easily, and two bombs got her close to the bows and practically blew them off. We've put airlocks over the holes and pumped out the forward compartment. They should be busy with the second now, and if the rest of the hull is water-tight, they might manage to find the safe. If not, there's no time.

'Simple as that, Easter. I'm going to *Gruesome* in about twenty minutes. Care to join me, after you've had another drink?'

'I'd like to very much, but no more to drink, thank you.' I knew the strength of these clear whiskies, and pushed the glass aside. 'I'll just slip up and change while you finish yours and have that pipe.'

'Fair enough. Your room's right at the top of the stairs, and then first on your left. You can't miss it; very pleasant and airy as I said. When you come down, I'll lend you an oilskin. The wind's starting to blow up already.' He lit his pipe as I hurried out.

As Mrs MacDawlish had remarked, the quarters were very wee, and they were crammed with Ricks' belongings. Only in the centre of the room was it possible to stand upright, so I ducked my head and craned through the window. Below stood a rusty shack which must be the chapel, and beyond it I could just make out the dim shape of *Gruesome*'s mast swaying above the headland on the Atlantic swell. Beneath the frigate's hull, there might be the answer to a question: the big question. Not just the punishment of a traitor, but how to avert a national crisis.

Yes, somewhere at the bottom of that valley, called the Mouth of Canna, they must find the answer to where Tom Ryde had gone. It had to be that way; there was no other answer. The British and German Naval reports coincided too closely to be coincidental.

He had come to Scotland. Come here and brought something with him, and now the fruits of his coming were starting to grow. Already the prologue was over and the play had begun.

'EPIDEMIC OF MADNESS – MANIA INCORPORATED' ran two of yesterday's headlines, and panic was mounting. Seven people had been killed in the last three days. How much longer had we got?

I glanced at my watch. Five hours to midnight, and how long before the approaching storm? And that storm was on its way. There were more white flecks on the water, and ragged clouds piling up over the sea.

'Our great, grey mother,' the Irish writer had called the sea: 'The scrotum tightening sea.' James Joyce was dead, dead in Trieste with 'His left eye wake and its neighbour full of water, Man,' but Tommy Ryde was alive – alive and kicking, and somewhere in the womb of that grey mother they might discover what made him tick.

'Coming, Easter?' I was splashing tepid water over my face when Treecher's voice thundered in my ears, and I put on an extra sweater and hurried down to keep our appointment.

Gruesome's launch was waiting at a stone jetty about a hundred yards from the hotel, and we lurched towards it through the wind. Treecher growled at the sailors who helped him up onto her lurching deck and sat down heavily in the stern. In his sou'wester and oilskins he looked like an advertisement for somebody's sardines.

'I don't like it,' he said. 'Don't like it at all. Blowing up faster than I thought. Won't hold till morning, whatever those BFs at the Met Office say.' He leaned forwards and bawled at the petty officer in charge. 'Come on, coxswain, get her moving, or do you hope Mr Easter and I will get out and walk on the waters?'

'Aye aye, sir. At once, Admiral. Just waiting to see that you and your friend were comfortably settled.' The man smiled widely and I realized that, to the lower deck at least, Treecher was affectionately regarded as a character. 'Cast off forward, Smith. Let go aft, Nobby.'

As we rounded the headland, the coming storm seemed very close. The white flecks I had noticed from the window were enormous and threatening at water level, and the ragged clouds had become a solid line filling the entire horizon. Only *Gruesome* herself appeared motionless. The frigate resembled a grey island in the dusk, with huge cables strained fore and aft and a tangle of hoses and cables hanging over her side, like creepers. It was as if we had entered another, more peaceful world as the launch swung into the still water under her lea and came to rest alongside a rope ladder.

I watched Treecher leap for the rope with surprising agility and pull himself steadily upwards. I followed with less skill, banging against the side of the ship at every step, and reached the deck on my knees, to be hauled upright by Ricks and a grinning rating.

'Well, here we are, Tubby.' Treecher nodded at a tall, still youthful officer at his side. 'In for the kill, as they say, and this is the man who's put us to all the trouble. Captain Hawes – Mr Easter.'

'How do you do,' Hawes' eyes were very friendly, but there was a certain uneasiness about them. 'Shall we go to the chart room, Admiral? Lot of noise about here.' He motioned to the wind, the creaking cables and the clatter of a heavy pump forward, and then led the way up to the bridge.

'Ah, that's much better.' Treecher settled himself onto a revolving stool and eyed the chart table, the gleaming paint and the brass instruments with affection. 'Well, Tubby, how's it going?'

'Very well, sir, by and large. Under normal circumstances and provided the ship's papers are intact, there'd be little difficulty in getting 'em out. Only the first two compartments were flooded and the rest of the hull seems sound enough. They've pumped out the foul air now, and as soon as the next shift goes down, they can start cutting through the central bulkhead and sea urchins from the safe.' He stood with his back towards us, looking through a porthole. 'That is, if the chaps do go down, sir, and I'd like to ask Mr Easter a question, if I may? Thank you Admiral.' Treecher had grunted and Hawes turned to me.

'Mr Easter, I don't know whether you are a sailor or not, but

I must make the position quite clear. In roughly seven minutes, the present shift will return to *Gruesome*, and the next one take over. The men will work in the hull of that U-boat for exactly half an hour, and at any time during those thirty minutes the storm is liable to break. If that happens, and the wind reaches gale force, my duty will be quite clear. We are off a rocky and deeply shelving coast at anchor. If the wind hits us at more than sixty miles an hour, the anchors are bound to give way and I will have to save my ship. That means slipping the cables and taking *Gruesome* out to sea, leaving the divers to certain death. The chances of a gale striking during the next shift are about fifty-fifty, so what I want to know is this.' He raised his head and stared me in the eyes. 'Are those papers worth the risk of three men's lives?'

My mouth suddenly went dry. I couldn't answer for a moment. I looked at the sullen sea and the approaching cloud bank. I thought of everything I had experienced during the last few days. I was almost surprised to hear my voice speak. 'Yes, Captain Hawes, I'm afraid the papers are.'

'Very well. We've been told to co-operate with you.' His features became cold and hostile. 'The next shift will go down as scheduled.'

'Just a moment, Captain Hawes. There's one more thing. Though I can't tell you what the safe contains, I'll try to show how vital the papers are.' I was going crazy. My own voice wasn't speaking to him, I thought, but by Christ, it was. 'With your permission, I'd like to accompany the next party.'

'What!' Hawes took a step back as though I'd struck him. 'No, a good gesture, but I'm afraid I can't allow that.'

'Just a moment, Tubby.' His answer brought a flow of relief from me, but Treecher's voice soon put a stop to that. 'It is a good gesture – very good indeed.' He left the stool and stomped over to me. 'I know why he made it too. If those men were left behind, you'd feel like suicide, Easter. Life wouldn't be worth living. Tell me something. You're fit enough are you? Heart, lungs and liver OK?'

'Of course they are.' I was about to complain of a dicky

heart, diseased lungs and a fatty liver, but I didn't get a chance. The admiral pounded my shoulder with a fatherly fist that felt like a club. 'Yes, fit as a flea, and let him go, Tubby. Knew there was stuffin' in the young fellow. Nephew of old Elephant Easter, one of the best sea captains that this country ever boasted.' The Elephant eulogy was interrupted by the sharp peal of a bell, and Treecher's thoughts returned to duty. 'Get crackin', Tubby. That's the signal to change watches in three minutes, so take him along to the bo'sun and don't worry. If you have to leave him to drown, I'll accept full responsibility.'

* * *

Those three minutes were about the shortest and longest I've ever known. Hawes hurried me down to the streaming deck, where two sailors fitted me out with enormous weighted boots and a science-fiction type suit. One of them was a fund of useful information.

'Don't suffer from nervous indigestion, I suppose, sir. Not liable to vomiting, are you?' he asked. 'Know what you'll see when they open that bulkhead won't be pleasant?

'But don't let them worry you, sir. Don't give 'em a second thought. All you need to do is to follow Chief Petty Officer Maud, sir.' He nodded at a diver preparing to take the plunge from the side of the ship. 'We're dead above the sub, and it's all lit up down there. You'll see the airlock orl rite. Just climb up the ladder, and Jimmy Maud'll give you a hand off with yer helmet.

'OK, sir, and goodbye.' The helmet closed around my head, I smelled the sweet odour of oxygen and then the slings on my shoulders tightened. I rose from the deck and then came down into the dark, choppy water.

Diving is not an unpleasant experience, once you've got the hang of things, and I had had that experience. There is hardly any sign of movement or descent. The suit pressed against my body like a womb, and it was as though, in a second, all exterior existence had ceased and I was completely on my own. A rather enjoyable sensation, though it didn't last long. Maybe a couple of minutes, but they seemed like hours. Then the darkness ended and there were lights all around me. I sank into a bed of very white sand, and my hands clutched a wall of red rock in front of me.

I didn't realize that that rock was the submarine at first. There was something too natural about that huge shape, coated with shellfish and gleaming with rust. Not man-made at all, I thought, and then I saw the conning tower above me, and on my left a ladder ran up to a bulge of metal, which was not rusty: the airlock.

I unclipped the line from my shoulders and clambered up the ladder. My heavy boots made the ascent a sweat, but mercifully the outer door was open and I closed it behind me and waited. My knees sagged as the chamber was pumped dry. A second door opened and I was safely inside the U 1001.

'Arf a tick, sir.' A bearded face grinned at me as its owner unscrewed my helmet and then stopped to remove the weights from my boots. 'That's better, ain't it. You'll feel quite your old self in a moment, but get your breath back first.'

'Thanks.' I paused and looked around. We were in a long, narrow compartment, packed tight with corroded machinery, torpedoes and bunks. There were dead fish on the deck, and from one of the bunks a naked human arm protruded, picked clean of flesh and sinew.

'Welcome to the crew's sleeping quarters, sir. The House of Lords, as the Jerries called it.' The beard grinned. 'The bomb got 'er over there, had to seal the bitch up with epoxy resin, before pumpin' 'er out.' He pointed at the bulkhead, and I saw that there had once been a gaping hole which was now filled with plastic. 'The others are cutting into Number 3, right now, sir, so would you like to have a squint?' He broke off as a bell rang and a loudspeaker burst into life.

'This is the captain speaking, and here are your final orders. Number 3 compartment is not known to have been flooded, and when you have gained an entry, commence your search for the safe. You will probably find it in the control room, just aft of the conning tower ladder. As soon as the safe has been released and secured to a line, you will leave the submarine and get out quick.

Leave all equipment behind and hurry things up. Speed is essential at this stage. Is that clear?'

'Message fully understood, sir.' My bearded pal spoke into a microphone. 'Cutting operations are now in progress. We should be through the bulkhead within five minutes.' He switched off the set and grinned at me. 'Let's get crackin', sir. The old man's starting to become edgy. The weather's blowing up. Don't want to pile *Gruesome* up on a fuckin' rock.'

'Cor, Gawd help sailors, on a nite like this!' He spat on the slime of the deck and hurried aft down a long corridor. More rusty litter on every side, more human skeletons, a crab scurrying between my feet, but at last the blue glow of an acetylene torch.

'Ah, Mr Easter.' Petty Officer Maud had also removed his helmet and was supervising the operations. He had blue eyes, very blond hair and a squint. 'The steel is three inches thick, but Dusty Miller should be through in a minute or two, and then . . .' He paused and stared at the widening amber circle in the metal. 'Then Miller and Brett will hook it and be damned quick too.

'You know what's behind that door, I suppose, sir?'

'Yes,' I said, but Maud didn't need an answer. He didn't even want one. He just stared at the glowing circle and waited till the ends met. 'Right, Dusty – Right, Brett. Off you go.' Maud raised his boot and kicked the metal. The circle tilted as though on hinges and toppled forward – the way ahead was clear. 'I'll go first, Petty Officer,' I shouted as the two men stepped aside, though I've no notion why. I do remember that the metal was still hot and I could feel the heat through my gloves as I gripped the edges. I stumbled on the deck but didn't actually fall; the deck was dry.

The dryness seemed strange at first. Not damp slime, but firm, clean metal was under my feet and that seemed wrong – that and the air. The air hissing from *Gruesome*'s pumps had a sweetish tang, but the atmosphere inside the compartment was dead and cold and had no smell at all.

'Hold on, Mr Easter. Have a light on in a tick, so stay still.' I heard Maud's voice, I saw the beam of his torch, I saw the things that had been hidden, and I tried not to scream.

I should have known, of course. Should have realized that the lack of oxygen and moisture would preserve the bodies, but not like this. My God, I'd never imagined it could be like this, and I remembered what an old man had told me years ago. The man had been a member of a salvage crew that had entered the wreck of a U-boat, off Marseilles, and he described his experiences vividly. I hadn't believed him. I couldn't believe that hell was like that.

No, not like that. Once I had seen a picture about the loss of a British submarine. I remembered how, when all hopes of rescue vanished, the actors died. They had bowed their heads, listened to a prayer reading by the chaplain and waited peacefully for the end. The cameras had drawn away from those peaceful, relaxed faces. The hull had become transparent and we had a view of them calmly grouped together when the film ended.

No, not like this. I had enjoyed the picture once; been rather moved by it. But now, I would have liked to have burned every inch of the celluloid as I looked at the reality.

'You are standing at the very base of the world,' I heard a voice say. 'Wherever you go, you may not go any deeper, because this is the worst place of all; the very base of the world.'

'Don't look at the pore bleeders, sir. Just concentrate on finding that safe.' Maud's normal tone interrupted the voice of my imagination. 'In the control room, just aft of the ladder, the skipper said it should be, and 'ere we are.' He pushed past me, and his torch lit up a tiny cell-like compartment. 'Yes, there's the bleeder, sir, but Christ! The bastards have welded it to the bulkhead.

'You stay here, and I'll go back for the cutter, sir.' He left me the torch and stumbled off, flinging equipment aside to give himself room to move the oxy-acetylene cylinders. The beam of his lamp showed me that he was right. The safe hung above a table on four riveted studs, and their heads were welded to the metal. Under the box was a photograph of a blonde woman and two young children. 'With our blessings to U 1001 and all who sail in her,' read the inscription, though I didn't have time to make out the signature. Maud pushed past me and turned on the cutter.

'That's the first one, sir, and this shouldn't take us long.' The top left-hand nut had disintegrated and he turned his attentions to another. 'Run and get a line, Mr Easter. We'll get this bleeder up and go with her.'

I groped my way forwards. I found the long nylon rope, and then I paused. The microphone coughed and I heard an unfamiliar voice.

'Chief Petty Officer Maud, this is the forebridge speaking. Miller and Brett are now back on board, and you and Mr Easter are to follow them immediately, with or without the safe. We are releasing the cables in five minutes and that is an order.'

'Hurry up, sir.' I was terrified. I wanted to hook it through the airlock double quick, but Maud called me back. 'Almost free now, Mr Easter, so hook the line through the handle, and listen carefully. There's another cable outside the lock, and we've got to drag this bitch out and clip 'em together. Understood?' The last bolt gave way as I tied on the rope and the safe clattered onto the deck. 'Right – pull.'

I won't bother to describe how we managed to get the safe out, except to say that it was bloody hell at first. We had to haul and manhandle the thing bodily across the dry deck and through the hole in the compartment. After that, progress was slightly easier. The safe slid like a sleigh on the slime, though the loudspeaker messages didn't help matters. 'God bless – Goodbye – God speed,' they kept repeating, which failed to cheer me on, but at last we were inside the airlock.

'Never mind about the helmets, Mr Easter,' Maud instructed, fumbling with the outer catch. 'Take a deep breath, hold tight onto me and pray that I can connect the cables.' He switched on his microphone and bellowed, 'Right, you stupid sods. Mission completed, so get us up fast.' He opened the second door and reached out.

I haven't a clue how we made it. The line jerked like a whiplash, dragging us forward. My back was rammed against the side of the submarine, and for a moment I almost lost my grip on Maud's suit and toppled back. Then we were clear and rising like a lift through the darkness, with a terrible pain racking my chest. I felt fresh air on my face and breathed deeply. Only for a moment, though. I toppled down onto something hard and unyielding and I passed out.

When I came round, I was on *Gruesome*'s deck, as with slipped cables she tore out to sea, and Maud's face was squinting beside me, till another face, black, glowering and angry came between us.

'Well, Easter, you've certainly taken your bloody time getting here,' said Admiral Treecher.

CHAPTER ELEVEN

'Therefore, upon receipt of these instructions issued on behalf of Grand Admiral Karl Doenitz, you are hereby requested and required to carry out this assignment with all due expedition.' Although the German Navy was of more recent growth than the British, its official documents appeared to be equally archaic. Kirk pushed the sheet of foolscap aside and grinned at his audience.

'Well, ladies and gentlemen,' he said. 'These are the papers found in the U-boat's safe, and I have asked you here mainly out of courtesy. Also, because you are all directly involved in this business.' He looked at Molly and me in our seats by the window. At Dr Helen Grace sitting on a *chaise longue* with her legs crossed. At Admiral Hugo Treecher busily preparing to light his pipe.

'You, Dr Grace, as you represent the hospital where at least one of these murders originated. Bill Easter, because he got the safe up for us. Mrs Bloom, for some valuable research work she has recently completed. Admiral Treecher, on account of his friendly co-operation.' He watched Treecher apply a match to his pipe and his smile faded. 'Now, Bill, what's the present score to date?'

'Eighteen, General. There was another couple in Liverpool this morning.'

'Thank you, my boy.' The old boy gave me an encouraging nod. 'That is eighteen murders during the last ten days, as far as we know. Murders which were almost always followed by the suicide of the attacker. Manic killings, because there was always a history of mental illness about the murderer, and something about the victim which aggravated the condition. That was the surface motive for all those acts, and it tells us nothing – nothing at all. As far as we are concerned, they are all murders without rhyme or reason, and it is up to us to find the reason – the where, why and how of it.' He paused and stared at our faces. 'Yes, my friends, and the first point is easily answered. In this very room, when I hired a ghost writer to check the text of a manuscript I had prepared for publication. The writer died near Canterbury, his murderer committed suicide after destroying my manuscript. They don't matter, but tell me something, Dr Grace. Does the name Joel Loser convey anything to you?'

'Loser – Joel Loser. Let me think for a moment, General Kirk.' A slight furrow spread across her homely face. 'Yes, the name conveys a little. Not much, but I think Loser was a zoologist, and he wrote a treatise on animal communication. Migratory instincts, extrasensory perception, that kind of thing.

'I read his paper, of course, long ago. There was a great deal about telepathic waves passed between communities of insects. All very interesting, but I don't believe his theories would hold water today.' She paused and the furrow deepened. 'Is that the man you mean, General?'

'Possibly, Doctor, though it might be a woman, as the name Joel may fit either gender. But, let's go back to the beginning and see what we can piece together, so far.' Kirk turned and massaged his hands before the fire. 'Early in 1944, our opponents across the North Sea had a rather jolly idea. They felt it would be an excellent thing if certain undesirable persons, such as the Allied leaders, were removed by assassination. At first, they considered using professional killers, but the risk of capture was too great. Professionals spill the beans, under torture, and real, dedicated fanatics were needed. In the end, they decided on psychopaths.

'No, not a very pleasant thought, is it, Admiral?' He watched Treecher blow his nose violently. 'All the same, it happened. A number of patients were selected from various asylums, and a research station was established on the Bodensee for their training – I use *training*, for the lack of a better word, but the point is this, Dr Grace. The officer in charge was our old friend the zoologist, Joel Loser.'

'But, I don't understand, General.' Helen Grace appeared baffled by the information. 'What could Loser have achieved?'

'I don't know yet, Doctor, but may I go on?' His eyes suddenly looked very old and tired. 'At about the same time that this place on the Bodensee was being established, an English traitor named Thomas Ryde was engaged in propaganda broadcasts from the German radio to this country. Ryde also did a good deal of work in POW camps. Yes, Admiral Treecher, as you say, the bastard!

'We know a great deal about Ryde nowadays, and he was a bad man. Probably the only really evil man who has come my way, though he had one interesting quality, and everyone who met him says the same. When you were with Ryde, he seemed able to exert a form of influence which made you feel important and self-righteous. Also, you wanted to please him in every possible way. Possibly a form of impersonal hypnosis, but it was there all right. That was why he was so useful to them on the radio and in the camps.

'Well, during '44 Ryde suffered a mental and physical decline, and he was injured in a bar brawl on the Reperbahn. His duties on the radio ended, and his colleagues were informed that he was dead, but that was incorrect. He was in fact transferred to that establishment on the Bodensee and placed in the care of our friend Loser.

'Those are the facts, my friends, and the rest is supposition, based on guesswork and Mr Easter's powers of detection.' It was my turn to receive a faint smile. 'The research station was bombed by the RAF later, and all the records were destroyed.

'But, Ryde survived, unfortunately. In April 1945 Thomas Ryde was seen near Bergen, being put into a U-boat.'

'A U-boat, General?' Treecher interrupted him excitedly. 'You mean the 1001 which we managed to cut up for you?'

'Yes, Admiral, the U 1001 from which you removed the safe for me.' He gave Treecher the ghost of a grin and opened a folder. 'You have heard the contents of the first sheet of orders which is signed by the officer commanding the Norway area.

'The next is far more interesting and was addressed to *Kapitan zur See* Hans Richter, who assumed command of the U 1001 during the same month. A most gallant officer Richter seems to have been. Two hundred thousand tons of Allied shipping to his credit.

Knight's Cross in 1943 – oak leaves and diamonds, the following year. Now, please excuse my rather quick translation.' He cleared his throat and proceeded to read aloud.

'"My dear Richter,
    By now you will have reached Bergen and taken over command of the U 1001. I am personally more than sorry to have had to ask the Grand Admiral to send you his enclosed orders, but it is imperative that the ship is commanded by a man in whom we have utter faith and confidence.
    It now seems clear that our troops and the Führer have been cut off and encircled in Berlin, and it is up to us to bring pressure on the enemies and force them to grant our unhappy Fatherland a just and honourable peace.
    Your mission, my dear Richter, concerns such pressures, though I fear that I cannot give you full details. Here, however, are your orders.
    As soon as the plane carrying the cargo and our agent reaches Bergen, you will take them aboard and proceed to a point off the north-west corner of Scotland: (Position: 4.78 degrees west – 8.1 degrees north.) Weather forecast and the latest Intelligence reports regarding minefields are attached.
    Having reached this position, you will lie submerged till 5 a.m., Greenwich Mean Time, 28 April, and then surface and convey your passenger and the cargo ashore. At the corner of the cliff marked X on the enclosed chart, you will find a road. At exactly 6.30 a.m., you will find a van waiting at the point of the road nearest to the sea. You will approach the van's driver and ask him his name. If he replies 'Mr James O'Brien', you will leave your passenger and the charge with him.
    Once this mission is completed, you are at liberty to take your command to any port still in the hands of our forces. If necessary, you may surrender her to the enemy. It is essential, however, that neither your officers nor your crew know the nature of the cargo in question.
    Believe me, *Herr Kapitan zur See*, I much regret sending you

on this mission which may cost you your life, but I am assured it is necessary, for both the Party and the Reich."

'End of message, ladies and gentlemen, and please excuse the rough translation.' Kirk tucked the paper back in its folder. 'The writer closes the note with *"Sieg Heil"* and adds his own signature: "Heinrich Himmler, *Reichführer, SS."*'

For a moment there was dead silence in the room, and then came the voice of loud, arrogant, down-to-earth reality. 'Cargo the chaps weren't told about, eh? Sounds melodramatic and slightly sinister.' Treecher lolled back in his chair with the pipe between his lips. 'Well, General Kirk, what was the cargo? Some sort of bomb or destructive device. Kind of secret, nuclear weapon?'

'In a sense, Admiral, but not quite what you think. The Nazis never had atomic weapons, thank God, but they may have created something just as bad. I believe Tom Ryde was landed from that sub; Ryde or the thing he had become.'

'Had become?' Treecher removed his pipe and snorted. 'Do you mind explaining yourself, Major General? I can't speak for the others, but what you say is completely beyond me.'

'I'm sure it is, Admiral, but I'm afraid I can't explain myself. That must be done by an expert, and the expert is in the next room, studying the facts now.' He smiled at me and Molly. 'That is why Mrs Bloom couldn't go to Scotland with you, Bill. She went to Paris to contact an old friend and bring him back with her.' He opened a door and called out. 'If you are ready, perhaps you would come through, Professor Darnley.'

I'd seen pictures of Professor Claude Darnley before, but I felt mirth rising as I looked at the reality. The man was only half dressed, though above the waist all was well. The mass of iron grey hair was a trifle long but neatly combed. The heavy, intellectual face was closely shaven, and the steel-rimmed spectacles were not ostentatious. Below the face, he wore a stiff white collar, a dark blue tie and a double-breasted jacket with a carnation in the buttonhole. From the waist up, he could have been a city businessman, but at the waist, Darnley's compromise with society ended. Under the jacket was a very short Highland kilt and a pair of heavy brogue boots. He looked like the product of a child's game of 'Heads and Bodies'.

'Well, I don't think there's any need to tell anybody why Mrs Bloom and I asked Professor Claude Darnley to help us.' The man bowed, as Kirk introduced him. 'Till last year, the professor held a chair at Edinburgh University, but recently he has been engaged in research work at the Sorbonne. Right, Professor, you've been through the facts as far as we know them, so may we hear your conclusions?'

'One minute, Major General. 'Fraid I'm out of this.' Treecher sat bolt upright, staring at Darnley's legs. 'Sorry, but I don't know who your guest is. Seen a picture of – of his face somewhere, but got no idea about his line of country.' With great difficulty, he raised his eyes and looked at Darnley's face. 'Seen a photograph of you somewhere, but that's all I can really say.'

For a moment, Darnley appeared to be deaf. He took off his glasses and polished them with the hem of his kilt. He replaced them on the end of his nose and studied Treecher with the air of a scientist examining an interesting laboratory specimen.

'You do not know, M'sieur l'Admiral? You cannot say, then let me tell you.' Darnley's voice was a strange mixture of Anglo-Saxon and Gallic. 'On my father's side, I can trace direct descent from Lord Henry Stuart – Earl Darnley. My mother is a blood relation of Louis Quatorze, *Le Roi Soleil*. I myself am the expert, the man at the top, the Maestro, the one who knows.'

For a moment Treecher seemed in danger of a stroke. His face took on a purplish tinge, he clenched his hands together, and a strangled, groaning sound came from his lips. Kirk attempted to pass over the incident.

'Perhaps I should explain, ladies and gentlemen. Professor Darnley is a member of the *Institut National* at the Sorbonne, specializing in mental health. He is also the author of a number of standard works on extraphysical phenomena. He is the master in the sense that he is one of the world's foremost authorities in that field.'

'Thank you, General Kirk, and after these interruptions may we get down to business?' Darnley took a sheaf of papers out of his jacket pocket. 'When you first telephoned me, I was naturally sceptical about the whole affair. But when Mrs Bloom called at my lodgings, I became rather pleased.' He smirked at Molly, and I felt like kicking the brute up his kilt. 'I always enjoy a trip to London in pleasant company and at another person's expense.' He laid down his notes and squinted at them. 'Now, however, I am really interested. Very interested indeed.

'Yes, I always thought I might one day locate the area, but it seems somebody has beaten me to it.'

'The area!' Kirk raised his white bushy eyebrows. 'Could you be more specific, please?'

'I apologize, General; partly talking to myself. I mean the area of the brain which controls these things. Things which are known to exist, but nobody understands them. Telepathy, in fact, my friends. A communication which requires no physical transmitter but can be as clear as day, and travel endlessly. There are too many cases to doubt its powers, but no one knows really how it works.

'No one up to now, that is.' He moved to the desk and sat down. His legs dangling over the edge looked ridiculous, but there was suddenly nothing amusing about him. 'Today we are inclined to laugh at the beliefs of primitive peoples. We talk of savages and mumbo-jumbo and the Dark Ages. We sometimes think that the Ancient Greeks were the first civilized race because they were free from superstition.

'In nearly every case we are right, and I repeat *nearly*. Let's dismiss ninety-nine per cent of the Negro witch doctors, the medieval sorcerers and the fakirs, as impostors, and what do you have?

'One per cent, which we cannot dismiss. Which makes us wonder. If we find that that single instance is proven, then . . .'

'Then what, Professor?' He had paused to clear his throat, and Dr Grace prompted him. 'Please go on, sir.'

'Then, Madame, the point is proven. The witch doctor can harm his victim without physical contact. The medieval sorcerer's doll is not a fairy tale but a real force. A man may wither from a curse as his ship nears land.' He paused again and produced a packet of Gauloises from his pocket. 'Yes, it may exist, this force. Communication without contact – without the senses being involved. And more than that – much more . . .' He lit the cigarette from a book of matches that I saw came from a club in the Rue Pigalle. 'If all that is granted, we have real power. Possession of the personality – the soul. Control of the unconscious becomes a real force.'

'But how, Professor Darnley?' Kirk had been taking notes, but he laid down his pen and looked up. 'How does this phenomenon fit in with Ryde and these recent killings?'

'I don't know, General. I honestly do not know, but I suspect. For most of my life, I have been studying this phenomenon, and there is one basic difficulty.' He dragged at his cigarette in an effort to concentrate. 'You see, this thing follows no known laws, and unlike other means of communication, there is no centre of the brain to transmit it. Speech, sight and touch have all been pin-pointed, but not telepathy. We have tried to explain it in many ways; some form of time sequence, for example, but we have never succeeded. Perhaps this Dr Loser used a much simpler method and found the answer.'

'But what, Professor?' Molly asked. 'What method might he have used?'

'My dear Mrs Bloom, I have no idea, but I suspect. Surely it is possible that this man Loser used vivisection.' He left the desk and crossed to a window. 'Yes, simple surgery on a living subject. A knife might have found the area of the brain which controls these things, and why not? The brain controls everything else, even our emotions and conscience. If he had discovered the centre responsible, the rest would be easy. He would expand the area and strengthen it, though I'm not sure how.' Henry Darnley looked down at the traffic crawling below. 'Injections perhaps, ultra violet, or radiation; we cannot say. He would kill more than half his experimental subjects probably, but so what? If one of them lived and was a person like Ryde – Tom Ryde, potential telepath already, a carrier of this force before treatment started, then ça va. You might get a situation very similar to what you have written there, General Kirk.'

'Thank you, Professor.' Darnley had turned and was staring at the papers on the desk, and Kirk nodded. 'That is very clear, but there are two further points I would like to know.

'Firstly, can this form of communication work both ways? You see our – enemies appear to be always one jump ahead of us. I send a man to Europe, and he is stabbed to death on the train from Dover. His murderer then commits suicide.

'Virtually the same thing happened to Mr Easter and Mrs Bloom in Berlin. Brenner tries to speak to them and then he dies, and the killer follows suit. It almost seems as though they were killed to stop them talking.'

'And why not, General? Granted one thing, the other is simple. Thought-reading would occur too. Why, there are adepts in Australia who claim that they can read another man's mind in over five hundred miles of space.'

'Your second question, please.'

'The time lag, Professor Darnley. It is almost forty years since Ryde disappeared, so if what you say is correct – if he became a carrier, why didn't he act sooner?'

'How can we know that, General? We can only guess what treatment was used on him.' Darnley returned to the desk and thumbed through the papers. 'Yes, before he was taken to the Bodensee, he became ill, didn't he? Drink and drugs and fighting in bars. An ice pick pierced his hand and left a scar, resembling a stigmata.

'And after the Bodensee period, he was probably paralysed, I suspect. Yes, here we are.' He had found the sheet he wanted and brandished it in Kirk's face. 'Himmler doesn't refer to him as a man but as a *cargo*. Captain Richter was to hand over the agent and his charge to a man named James O'Brien.

'I believe that answers you, General. Whatever was done to him left the mind and the body paralysed and weak. Maybe it took him nearly forty years to recover, but he'd only be in the early sixties now. If he found his powers, I don't think it would take him long to use them.'

'And the fact that it is only the mentally unbalanced who have been affected so far, Professor?' Molly asked the question nervously and received a sharp answer.

'My dear Mrs Bloom, you are not, to my knowledge, a psychiatrist, and surely the point is obvious.' Darnley looked at her with disapproval. 'In certain forms of mental ill health there is a vacuum in the brain which is very liable to suggestion. How easy for this thing to creep into the vacuum and control it.

'Also, remember what Ryde was like originally. General Kirk described him as a truly evil human being, so try to imagine what was done to him on the Bodensee. He must have been subjected to some form of treatment which almost destroyed his brain and his body. Surely, when he recovered, he might feel a kinship with the mentally sick. A desire to take over crippled minds and merge them with his own. It might also be a practice ground – a form of sport.

'Yes, sport, General Kirk.' He frowned at the interruption. 'He might need practice and relaxation, and half the cases seem to have been purely childish and illogical. While the others were clever and well thought out. I believe that we have two sides of a personality to deal with. One is that of a retarded boy, and the other a genius.'

'Thank you, Professor. That is more or less what I needed to know.' Kirk looked at Darnley's cigarette and then reached for his cigar case. 'Any idea how this thing can be stopped?'

'That is your job, *mon général*, but there is only one way in my opinion. Find this creature which was once called Thomas Ryde. Find him and destroy him quickly.' Darnley gathered up his notes and started to stuff them back into his pocket. 'And I stress the need for speed. At every moment we sit chatting here, Ryde's powers are increasing. They are gaining strength and soon they may spread.

'To date, only one section of the community has been affected: the mentally ill, but that may not last. The sane and well-balanced may become possessed, and if that happens . . .' He stood up and I recognized his tartan.

'My ancestor, Henry Stuart Darnley, became the second husband of Mary, Queen of Scots. He was said to have been involved in a plot against Bothwell. He was definitely involved in the murder of Rizzio. He himself was blown up by gunpowder, probably with Mary's knowledge and consent.

'Gunpowder, ladies and gentlemen. A puny explosive by today's standards, but effective enough at close quarters, and what I want to say is this.' He moved and the Stuart kilt brushed against Kirk's knees.

'If Tommy Ryde is alive, General, you're bound to find him, but this is what matters. Remember that the original Nazi plan was to liquidate all the Allied leaders at the end of the war, and Ryde was intended to carry out this aim.

'Gunpowder against nuclear fission, General Kirk. The choice is yours. You'd better find Tom Ryde quickly, or else . . .' He paused by the door and smiled, with his fingers on the knob. 'Or else you'll have something on your conscience to make an outbreak of mild 'flu look more lethal than an epidemic of bubonic plague.'

CHAPTER TWELVE

'Damnation.' Grace and Darnley had departed and Kirk sat at his table, puffing at a cigar and glowering at us. 'How did that damn feller know about that damned conference? Was he just guessing perhaps? Reading the PM's mind, or was he sure? Had someone told him about the business?'

'What business?' I said, because I didn't know what he was talking about. 'What damned conference?'

'No harm in telling you two, I suppose. Public knowledge soon, if that chap Darnley spreads the word. *Meeting of the Minds of the World's Top People.*' He blew his nose, and snorted. He explained and my spirits sank even further when I understood.

In her own ineffable way the Prime Minister, Mrs Hecuba Racher, had decided to strike a blow for world peace, and peace could only start at the top. The leaders of the earth's leading countries had been approached and they were all quite willing and eager to talk and most grateful for Mrs Racher's kind invitation. Their numbers included the Presidents of France and the United States, the Head of the West German Bundestag, the Chairman of the Soviet Union and the Chairman of the People's Republic of Red China. This quintet would assemble at Chequers in twenty-four hours' time. They would arrive at separate airports and be driven to Chequers in secrecy. If, under the motherly eye of the Prime Minister, these gentlemen didn't immediately decide to cast their swords into ploughshares, Mrs Racher was not the woman she thought she was, and she might be right. But . . .

But if Professor Darnley was also right, I saw breakers ahead. No gibbering idiot would rush in brandishing a knife to threaten the Assembly. The threateners would come when the guests were already there. An American CIA man with a gun. A KGB agent bearing a bomb. A British waitress offering more of that delicious mushroom soup they had all enjoyed so much. The gathering would depart in peace, and chaos might follow.

Might follow – wrong tense: it bloody well would. I remembered a remark attributed to Einstein. Someone had asked the ancient sage what weapons would be used in the Third World War, and the sage replied that he was sorry, he had no idea about the Third World War, but he was quite certain about the Fourth. 'The only weapons we can use will be rocks.'

'Yes, Bill; a pleasant thought, isn't it?' My expression and no mind-reading abilities revealed my thoughts to Kirk. 'Not a peace conference but a preparation for destruction, and it's too late to stop the guests arriving now. Too late to check their bodyguards too, and equally useless. One British Air Force pilot could demolish Chequers with a few rockets.

'Now, who the hell is that?' In the distance, I heard a doorbell ring, but Kirk made no move to answer it at once. 'Damn!' he said. 'Wednesday, and the manservant's afternoon off. I'll just have to go myself.' He stomped off to welcome the visitor, and I thought of Molly and her uncle. Poor Molly Bloom, and wicked Tom Ryde, who had to be found and destroyed first. Destroyed before he wiped out the world's leaders and the world.

'This young gentleman wishes to see you, Mrs Bloom.' Kirk returned with a boy at his side; a boy I recognized. The last time I'd seen him, I'd booted him in the balls. 'Gives his name as Terry Triggs, and says his business is urgent.'

'But I don't understand, General.' Molly gaped at the lout, who was clutching a suitcase. 'What do you want, Terry? How did you know I was here?'

'I followed youse, Missus. Bin waitin' outside for over two hours and I got fed up. Something in 'ere that I have to show youse, Mrs Bloom.' Triggs' voice sounded strange and my muscles flexed automatically. 'An invention of me own, which might speed up the production line next term. Look for yourself, Mrs Bloom.' He lowered the case onto the floor, he stooped to open the catch, and then he reeled back, because I hit him. My good foot shot out and caught him on the edge of the jaw. His head slammed against the desk and Terry was out cold.

'Well, well, Bill. Quick thinking, but I hope you're right. Kicking a thirteen-year-old boy in the face could lead to serious charges.' The General ignored the unconscious Triggs, picked up the case and laid it on the desk. 'Now let's have a squint at this contraption. And don't touch the lock, Molly Bloom. If Bill is right, the lock stinks to heaven and we'll open the side first.' He produced a clasp knife and stuck the blade through the leather. Dark grey powder trickled through the gap, and he chuckled and lifted a morsel to his lips. 'Yes, just as I thought: gunpowder,' he said, after tasting the stuff. 'Almost as much as blew Darnley's infamous ancestor to Kingdom Come and just as deadly.' He enlarged the hole, tilted the thing sideways and shook out a great pile of powder. 'Well, that should be safe enough, and we'll take a look at the detonator.' He pressed the lock, there was a sharp click, the top opened and we saw a tiny flame glowing. 'Congratulations, Bill. Never thought you had the brains, but there we are.' He blew out the flame, and I saw that there was an ordinary cigarette lighter attached to the back of the lock with adhesive tape. 'Press this catch and a lever presses the lighter. The flame goes on, the gunpowder explodes under pressure and down goes cradle and baby and all.

'Now, tell me about baby, Molly.' He scowled at the recumbent figure on the floor. 'I gather Master Triggs was a pupil of yours at Carthage Road School, and that suggests he's a half-wit, but what else is there to say? Neurosis, mental ill-health, suicidal tendencies?'

'No.' She bent over Triggs. 'Terry was rather a clever boy by our standards. A bit of a hooligan, of course, they mostly are, but good with his hands and obedient enough by and large.'

'Good with his hands, eh?' Kirk glanced at the pile of powder on the desk. 'Yes, I suppose that that infernal device proves your point, and it also suggests that Darnley could be right. If Bill hadn't clobbered Triggs, we'd have died several minutes ago, and the mechanical genius with us.

'But no known tendency towards *felo de se*. Very curious, because he'd have been the first sane individual to receive the first blast of the trumpet. And obedient, eh? Ready to talk to you and his school pals.' He watched Molly nod and crossed to a cabinet. 'Well, Bill, we'll just have to see that the blighter talks to us, and I've got an excellent tongue-loosener in here. Sodium pentothal – the Russian Truth Drug.'

'General Kirk, you cannot use such a thing.' Molly still crouched over Triggs like a protective mother hen. 'I don't know how this boy found me here, or why he brought those explosives. I don't know why he hated me, but he's suffered enough and needs hospital treatment – not torture.'

'Who said anything about torture, my dear?' Kirk was filling a syringe from a purple-coloured bottle. 'To the best of my knowledge the effects of pentothal are more pleasant and restful than otherwise and they do little permanent harm. Terry should be round in a few minutes, and when we've had our little chat, we'll see about a hospital.'

'Excuse me, please, Mrs Bloom.' He knelt down beside her and rolled up the boy's sleeve. 'Wish me luck, Billy,' he said. 'And pop goes the weasel.'

The piston plunger had been driven home, but for a moment nothing happened. The drug had entered Terry's blood stream, but there was no visible reaction. The clock on the mantelpiece ticked on, but the eyes didn't flicker. Kirk gripped his wrist and the pulse remained steady. For a full five minutes there was no change at all, and then I heard Kirk speaking.

'Your name is Terry Triggs, my boy, and I wish to know more about you. A great deal more, so open your eyes and look at me.' Like a miracle, the lids fluttered, and they did open. 'Wider, please, Terry. Ah, that's better and listen carefully. I'm a friend and I want to help you.' The old Judas sounded perfectly genuine and quite friendly. 'Now tell me, Terry Triggs, how did you come here, and why did you bring a bomb to kill us?'

'Bomb – bomb.' The voice was indistinct and almost too low to be heard at first. 'I made the bomb long ago to put into Mr Harrison's car, but the bleeder left – left years back with a nervous breakdown and I never got the chance.'

'Didn't want to harm you or Mrs Loom, General Lurk, nor Mr Beaster either. Just had to follow instructions like what the geezer said.'

'What geezer, Terry?' Kirk hadn't liked the misuse of his name, and his own voice was much less friendly. 'Who told you to bring that bomb here?'

'The gentleman, like I said. He told me Missus Bloom would be here and so she was. Waited outside for well nigh two hours, I did, Mr Chirk, and then got fed up and rang your bell. Just about to show her the present, when Mr Easter went and clobbered me.'

'My name is Kirk, son. Major General Charles Kirk, and don't forget that again.' The old pompous tone was icy now. 'A man sent you here to kill Mrs Bloom. To kill me and Mr Easter and yourself, Terry, so tell me about him. Did he also have a name? Can you describe him?'

'No, but his hand was sort o' scarred like. Looked as though someone had once putter – knocked er – stuck er spike through it.'

'Mr G.R., Billy.' Kirk looked at me and then resumed the interrogation. 'And where did you meet this fellow, Terry?'

'On the cliffs, it was, Charles. Last Saturday – at night. Marty Soames came with me, Charles, but he was scared o' the dark. Scared stiff by them lions and tigers in the garden, and them chaps on the roof. Poor Marty ran away, but I wasn't scared. He ran away and I went in, and they took me down to see the man with the funny hand. He told me what to do – what I still have to do . . .' Triggs broke off in a fit of coughing. 'But, water, sir. For God's sake, gimme a mug o' water.'

'Quickly, Bill. On the sideboard.' Kirk muttered and I sprang into action to obey orders. I reached the sideboard, I found a jug and I started to fill a glass. I never finished the errand of mercy, however. Molly suddenly screamed, Kirk cursed and the boy gasped. I swung round and saw that the sodium pentothal demonstration was over. Kirk had been reaching in his pocket to show the victim something of interest. The victim had seen the knife that the old fool had placed on the desk. Terry Triggs had grabbed the knife and sliced his throat open. The mad eyes were closed forever.

* * *

'No, not a nut, Billy, though somewhat feeble-minded, one might say.' There was no point in summoning a doctor or an ambulance at this stage, because Terry Triggs was dead, and Kirk had watched Molly make a telephone call and pick up the receiver, to make another.

The first call had been to Triggs' mother and not to inform her that Triggs was dead; merely a simple enquiry as to where her son had been last Saturday night and the answer was equally simple. 'At 'ome, watchin' the tele.'

Molly's next source of information seemed equally useless, and I heard a strident female voice rattling her eardrums. 'Why, Mrs Bloom, me and young Marty was up on the moor visiting his Dad. Like we do every third Saturday of every bleedin' month.'

'The moor? Dartmoor, of course. My Jim's doing fifteen years there, and I didn't know there was another.'

'Nah, Marty wasn't out of me sight for more than a couple of minutes, when he was in the lav.'

'Sure, you can ask the fuckin' governor or the chief screw, if you doubt me word, but I'll tell yer this, madam,' a pause and then indignation came pouring out, 'My Jim may have been a bad 'un, but I'm an honest woman I am. A fully paid-up member of CUNTS, which should make me a valued member of society.' She snorted at Molly's question. 'CUNTS, Mrs Bloom, stands for the Confederation of United Nationalized Transport-Supervisors, and I'm surprised that any educated woman didn't know as much.

'Nah, the bleedin' train didn't get back to the Smoke till well after twelve, and I had to queue for nearly an hour for a bleedin' taxi.'

'Thank you, Mrs Soames, and you've been most helpful.' Molly cut the woman short and replaced the receiver. 'No joy there either,' she said. 'Both boys were with their mothers all the time, so Triggs must have been lying.'

'And yet, the bomb was real enough, my dear. That boy intended to blow us up, and he was also told to commit suicide.' Kirk stared at the volumes on his bookshelves. 'On a cliff – lions and tigers in the garden and men on the roof. The place must exist somewhere, but where?' He strode over the dead boy's body and squinted at the shelves. 'Vera Sackville-West's *The English Country House*. J.A. Gotch, *The English Home from Charles I to George IV*. Neither of those will help, I know them too well, but this joker might. I only bought it a week or two ago.' He pulled out a heavy tome and carried it back to the desk. 'Yes, Banderton's *Threats, Follies and Fantasies*. That might possibly help.' He flicked through the early pages and frowned. 'I know Alnwick Castle has male figures on the battlements, stone men, but they were put there to make the Scots think the place was well defended. Let's see what Mr Banderton has to say on the subject of follies.

'Ah – Ahah! *Ecoutez moi, mes enfants*.' He had found a suitable reference and smiled. 'Yes, indeed, listen to this: "Nantmere Lodge; a Victorian folly, built by Sir Victor Nant around the turn of the century. There is no mere or lake nearby to account for its name, which is probably invented at the whim of its designer. Externally, the Lodge has little of architectural merit to recommend it to visitors, though in the grounds a number of animals of the carnivorous type are displayed, modelled life-size and in concrete. On the roof, stand or kneel statues of Sir Victor himself also life-size and armed with a rifle. Sir Victor Nant was a famous, or infamous, big game hunter, in his prime.

' "The interior of the residence can actually be described as infamous in every sense of the word, and shows that Sir Victor was mentally disturbed. Entrance could only be gained by crossing a moat surrounding the house, and the decorations might once have been explained as Gothic. Booby traps and see-through mirrors were said to have abounded, collapsible beds were provided for unfortunate visitors, and there were no living-in servants for obvious reasons. The basement had been fitted out as medieval dungeons, together with a torture chamber."' Kirk turned a page with relish. 'Ah, pity. It seems that old Victor caught typhoid in 1912 and died intestate. There were no claimants to his estate, and the

Lall was finally taken over by the local authorities during World War I. The place has been cleaned up and is used as a reception centre for sick children.' He looked up from the book and stared at Molly. 'What's that, dear? Why gasp? It's all there. Stone animals in the garden and a stone man up on the roof; if they're still there of course, and the council hasn't slung 'em out with the torture chamber, the collapsible beds and the drawbridge.'

'Sorry, General, but the address. Where is the place?'

'In Devon, about five miles east of Exmouth, actually, and on the coast as Triggs implied. But, so what? Do you know Nantmere Lodge, my dear?'

'As it happens, I do, General.' Molly leaned forward and took the book from him. 'And so did these two boys, Triggs and Soames. We had a school camp in Devon, the year before last, and they came with the party. Went scrambling on some rocks, and fell and cut themselves pretty badly.

'I was in charge at the time, and I drove them over to the Lodge to have anti-histamine injections against tetanus. Yes, that's the place all right, but it's wrong – completely wrong.' She had found an illustration and pointed at a lawn before the front of the building. 'When was this book published?' She turned to the frontispiece and nodded. 'Last year, and that makes Mr Banderton a ruddy liar, Bill.' She held up the illustration for my inspection, and I saw that there were three animals on display: a lion, a tiger and what might have been a grizzly bear about to wade into action.

'I was there in June, General Kirk, and there were no stone animals in the garden, and no men on the roof either. Anything to say to that?'

'No, my dear, and what you say is quite true. Look at the note beside the list of illustrations,' Kirk replied mildly. 'That photograph was taken five years before this book was published.'

* * *

The photograph was out of date – so what? A call to the Devonshire Constabulary assured us that the figures and Sir Victor's statues gave the children nightmares. They had to be removed; the nightmares continued.

'Maybe Sir Victor's ghost was wandering around the house and terrifying the children,' a council official had suggested. 'Surely a couple of exorcists could get rid of the spectre, cheaply?' A C of E canon and a Catholic priest were called in. They said prayers in every room and spattered the walls with holy water, but that didn't solve the problem. The force of evil increased.

Drains, decoration and damp! These might be responsible. The drains were relaid, the house was painted in a tasteful mixture of white and gold, and the damp-proof course was checked and rechecked. The work cost the council a great deal more than the exorcists had done, and the results on the good side were nil. Three suicides, one murder and two cases of mayhem persuaded the authorities that enough was enough. No more ratepayers' money could be squandered on Nantmere Lodge, and the house was empty. Its inmates had recently been transferred to other establishments. The folly stood, alone and forlorn on the cliffs, waiting for buyers, who failed to turn up.

'And can you blame 'em, sir?' The desk sergeant's voice had asked Kirk on the telephone. 'I can't, and I've been inside the dump. Nantmere Lodge has an atmosphere you could cut with a knife.'

Possibly the man was right, but what business was it of ours? No reason for us to gulp a quick supper in a pub, climb into Kirk's ancient Mercedes and be tearing down to the West, to glorious Devon, like a cat on heat.

Those were my views, but my companions didn't share them. As usual, I had been given the job of driving the car, and Kirk and Molly sat in the back discussing the situation with a mixture of glee and trepidation.

'It must fit, Molly,' Kirk kept repeating. 'All the murderers are tied together, and the knot is your uncle, Thomas Ryde. All inmates or patients, from nursing homes or mental institutions, and every one of 'em must have known Ryde or come under his influence.

'That chap in Berlin, Bill. What was his name again? Thank you. Count von Wessel, of course, killed Erik Brenner to stop him talking about the U-boat, and Wessel must have met your uncle in Germany during the war, Molly.

'But we found the U-boat, didn't we, and in an hour or so we should find Uncle Thomas or what's become of him.'

'Become of him!' Molly gave a little moan and, through the driving mirror, I saw that her face was deathly white. 'What exactly do you mean, General Kirk?'

'You heard what the feller Darnley had to say. Ryde was altered, wasn't he? He was sent to this country to carry out political assassination. Well, he failed then, but what about tomorrow at Chequers? Six heads of state will be sitting there, talking politics, and they may never know the killers are in position. Hypnotized killers, Bill. Individuals possessed by evil – controlled by the Devil.

'And the Devil will win, Bill, unless you get on a bit faster.' We were already past the Exeter bypass and doing about eighty, but the brute still demanded more speed. 'Take the next turn on the right, and then the second left should see us home, me son.

'No, Molly, I have no idea what your ancestor will be like, but I do know this. Tommy Ryde was an unpleasant individual – a bad penny to start with, and time and treatment won't have mellowed the blighter – not in the least. Try to be objective, Molly, and forget you're his niece, because, in a sense, you're not.' The old, domineering swine broke off and turned on me, because I'd neglected to fork right as ordered. 'Oh, Bill, you bloody, incompetent fool. Weren't you listening? Couldn't you understand a word I said?'

'Yes, General Charlie, I did understand, but I can also read a map, and this is the way. I took the second fork on the right, and then the second left, and there we are. The sea below, a hill in front – a house ahead.'

The illustrations had suggested that Nantmere Lodge was a large house, and the sergeant had implied that it looked gruesome; they were both wrong. The Lodge might be large, but under the moon there was nothing sinister or unattractive about it. A well-proportioned Victorian residence of red brick with lights shining in the porch and the ground floor.

'Ah, we have company, Bill, so stop here and let's go visit 'em.'

There was another car parked in the drive, so I drew up beside it and we climbed out. I followed Kirk and Molly across the gravel and across the moat which had been filled in. I watched Kirk ring the bell of the front door.

There was no reply and nothing happened. The battery might have been flat, the mechanism rusted up, but no sound came. Kirk waited for perhaps fifteen seconds and then tried the door handle. The door opened and we stepped inside Sir Victor's folly.

'Ah, good evening, General Kirk. It is rather late, but we've been expecting you. Haven't we, Doctor?' The light was dim and I didn't recognize the voice at first. Then I saw the speaker quite clearly, though he looked different. Dr Marton seemed smaller and older and his face had shrunk; there were dark lines under his eyes.

'You all know Helen Grace, of course, so come in and join the party, Mr Easter and Mrs Bloom. Do shut the door after you, please. Rather chilly for the time of year and there's a wind blowing outside.

'Ah, that's better.' I'd kicked the door to, and his tired eyes smiled. At his side, Helen Grace looked as brisk and methodical as always. Standing slightly behind them was a man whom I'd never seen before, though he looked familiar. 'May I introduce Mr Pettifer?' Marton said. 'He is the former caretaker of this establishment and has been showing us around. Most kind of him, and now shall we get down to the business in hand, General? The affair of Tommy Ryde?'

'Good – excellent.' Kirk had nodded and it was Pettifer who spoke. 'As a former chief of British Army Intelligence, General, you should be allowed into Chequers tomorrow, and there is your equipment.' He nodded at a small briefcase on a table. 'A rather more efficient device than that boy tried to use on Mrs Bloom, but that was a pure accident. Tommy tends to have rather an acid sense of humour at times.' Pettifer tended to have a rather rasping accent which got on my nerves, but not as much as Kirk's behaviour did. To think that the old boy was involved in a conspiracy! A Nazi plot to wipe out all the world's leaders, East and West! To create another war which might destroy the world! The truth was too shocking to contemplate, but it was there, all there. I only wished I'd had a recorder to tape it.

Tommy Ryde had been landed from a U-boat, and a keeper had come with him. The keeper's title was Dr Helen Grace or Fräulein Doktor Joel Loser. I didn't realize that the name Joel could apply to either sex then, but I knew the story. I pictured it in her face and imagined her in action. She and her cargo had been picked up by a van, possibly an ambulance, and driven south. The driver's name was Dr Marton, an English collaborator. Their destination was Nantmere Lodge, where Ryde had been looked after by another British traitor, the man called Pettifer.

That all fitted. Kirk's treason fitted. The old buster was due for death, but he probably didn't want to go out alone, with a bang instead of a whimper.

All clear, and only a few problems remained. Why had Molly and I been brought along to the Lall? Certainly not for the good of our health. And what had been done to Ryde? Why had he waited so long to take appropriate action?

I hadn't a clue, but it seemed I would soon find out. Grace-Loser had pressed a switch, and a trapdoor in the floor opened. I saw a flight of steps leading down, so I went down and the others followed me. Down into a little warm room that smelled of scent and flowers and something else I couldn't place. For perhaps the first time in my life, I felt completely at peace and happy. A difficult sensation to describe. Maybe like being a very young child again, though I won't try to explain my feelings, because Grace was speaking to Molly.

'Meet your uncle, Mrs Bloom,' she said. 'Behold the Man.'

Another panel had opened, she pointed towards it, and then, to my astonishment, Kirk fired. He had taken a Luger automatic from his pocket and he fired wildly and only twice. The first bullet slammed through Marton's forehead, the second pierced Pettifer's chest, and they both toppled backwards. I think they were both dead before they reached the floor, but I can't be sure. The pistol dropped out of Kirk's hand and he stared at me as though he was drugged. 'Pick it up, Bill,' I heard his voice say. 'Pick up that gun and kill him.'

I couldn't. I tried to bend towards the Luger, but my muscles seemed paralysed and my body wouldn't obey me. I just stood quite still and stared at the panel on the wall.

The panel was open and there was a face behind it. A huge bloated face, though the body beneath it was puny. A tiny body held upright by straps fixed to the sides of its cage; tubes penetrated the flesh to force nourishment and life into the brain above. An oddly childish face, though I knew that Tom Ryde was well over sixty. A face that had swelled out of all normal proportions; its flesh was pressing against the walls of its cabinet. A tortured face with eyes that flickered in agony and a mouth that gasped for air.

'No, General Kirk, Mr Easter can't reach the gun. He is completely helpless and a slave to that – the thing I made.' Helen Grace stooped and lifted the pistol. She pointed the muzzle at a chair and smiled as Kirk sat down. 'That's right, have a seat, make yourself comfortable and listen. Listen to me – the Prime Mover.' Her lips curled and she moved towards two metal cylinders and turned the taps. 'You came here to betray and destroy us, but I have the power now, and soon you'll feel it. You'll go to Chequers, General, and you'll take the case with you and then kill yourself. I gave Tom Ryde the powder to control human beings like you. We used ultra-violet rays to inflame his brain centres, and the centres responded. They worked on lunatics at first, and now they're working on you.' She paused and I saw that the eyes in the case had ceased to flicker. They stared at Kirk without any movement at all. 'Yes, it's starting now, General Kirk. Mr Easter can't move, but you can and you'll move when I tell you to.

'But not before – not till I give the word, my friend, so try to look away from him, if you can. That's not possible of course. We all have some private horror which cannot be resisted and soon I'll know yours.' She laughed at the poor old blighter sagging in his chair, and gave a few examples. 'Rats, spiders, impalement, or the fear of being buried alive. What's waiting for you in your Room 101, Charlie Kirk? We'll find out before long.' I saw Kirk grip the chair arms, to fight the pain. I saw him try to turn his head away. I saw him fail. I heard him whimper and then he slid forward. Somebody inside the panel moved.

'Yes, have a good look, Mrs Bloom. That's your uncle, all right, and we've no quarrel with you.' Grace watched Molly peer through the gap and she laughed again. 'You're one of the gang. Blood's thicker than water, and birds of a feather stick together.'

'But, not like that.' Molly didn't appear to hear her for a moment and then she did speak. 'No, uncle, not like that. I never thought you could have become like that.' Lies, to reassure herself, because Tommy Ryde was like that – just like that. That was the truth – what he had become. He had been brought home in a U-boat and placed in a lead-lined box. He smelled of scent and antiseptic and corruption, and a little amber light revealed everything.

Yes, everything. Like some obscene, fairground exhibit, Ryde hung from the straps of his cage with air roaring through his lungs, and the pierced hand clutching one of the grey tubes which forced nourishment into every aperture of his terrible little body.

And the face too – above all, the face. A face which was so changed but still remembered from old photographs in the albums. Vast now, in the swollen head which had absorbed its own bone structure and spread outwards, pressing against the sides of the cabinet that held it. That and the eyes – the same bright blue eyes Molly had seen years ago in photographs staring at her from their tortured sockets.

'No,' Molly whispered. 'You may be my uncle, but I have to stop you. We are the last members of the family and you're my sole responsibility. She stooped towards the cylinder taps, and then straightened as Grace clutched her arm. 'You,' she said. 'You made him like that, Dr Grace. Oh, I know that my uncle was a bad penny, a crazed, evil creature from the start, but you dared to do that to another human being.'

'Stop thinking on those lines, Molly.' The woman's own expression altered and she suddenly looked quite different. No longer a kindly governess or school teacher, but a jailer. The features changed too, and only a French term can really describe what I saw: *La Gueule*, the Muzzle of a Beast. The voice altered as well.

It sounded clipped and masculine, and the words had a drawl and a hint of Oxford behind them. 'You are quite right, my dear,' she said. 'You and Tom are the sole survivors of the family and you can't hurt me. Why should you wish to? I made him what he is, but he's taken over, and we're one flesh now.'

Maybe it was the voice that made me feel dizzy and lose my balance. Perhaps Ryde's staring eyes made me slip to the floor. I don't know, but I saw Molly hit her. She hit the woman with everything she had, and though Dr Grace tried to resist, she couldn't stop Molly Bloom. Molly struck Grace with her fists and her nails and the flat of her hands. She threw her to the ground and kicked her in the face when she tried to get up.

A moment later, Kirk was on his feet, and I saw that, as the woman fell, she had stumbled over the cylinder tubes and dragged them out from their sockets. A loud, hissing noise came from the taps, and behind the panel something screamed.

★ ★ ★

The General felt my pulse, and then he looked at Molly. Now that the fight was over, she looked stunned and ill, and her left cheek was bleeding. 'Well done, little lady. Quite a scrap, but are you all right?'

'I'm all right, General. For the first time I feel quite all right, but what about Bill?' She knelt over me, and her blood trickled down onto my chin. 'Bill – Bill, my darling, please look at me. That woman's dead, and you must forgive me.'

'Nothing to forgive, my dear, and don't worry about Easter. Fellow's got the constitution of an ox, and the story's finished.' That was Kirk's cynical reply, but he was wrong. The story hadn't finished.

With nourishment from the cylinders cut off, the thing in the case was trying to get out. It was straining against its straps, dying in agony, and had lifted its face through the door of the tomb. Its huge face, swollen and distorted and scarlet as it struggled for what had kept it alive for so long. Ryde's face was fully two feet across.

It filled the opening, with the blue eyes staring from their bursting sockets and the lips moving. 'I – I – I,' he repeated. Just 'I', while his skin turned from scarlet to purple to black, and each vein glowed and burned and became a luminous pipe. 'I wish,' he said, and then the face swelled outwards against the wall. At last, with the 'I's turning to screams, and a noise like tearing paper, the creature fell back and withered.

CHAPTER THIRTEEN

'I. The personal pronoun which denotes pride; the worst sin of them all.' We had moved up to Grace's study on the ground floor, and Kirk spoke, with a sheaf of her notes spread out before him. 'A pity that they're all dead, but this explains the process fully enough. Grace or Loser found the centres lodged behind the brain's frontal lobe and she was provided with an obvious subject for treatment.' He turned a page and nodded. 'Yes, Thomas Ryde was not just a bad penny; he was an egocentric as well, and he possessed the gift of hypnosis. A natural subject, as I said, and the hypnotic tendencies increased under ultra-violet ray treatment, though he probably suffered a great deal during that process.' The old, boring voice droned on and I looked through the window. Outside it was almost day, and I could see the sun rising over the Channel.

'Well, children, that appears to be that, and we can say goodbye to Nantmere Lodge. There could be a bit of a pong for a day or two, but the county council and the police can take care of that. There'll be no trouble at Chequers, which is what concerns me.' Before I could stop him, he leaned forwards and tossed the file onto the fire, which was still burning. The papers crumpled, turned orange and burst into flames.

'Oh, sorry, Bill. Did you want to keep Grace's notes and sell them to a collector of curios, or a mad doctor, who might copy the experiments and create more havoc?'

'No, my boy. That's hardly an Englishman's line of country – not cricket at all. Shall we get moving back to the smoke?'

'Would you drop me at the station please, Kirk?' For the first time, Molly spoke. 'Your car has had quite enough of me and my family already.'

'Why, my girl. Think you're too old for Bill? Well, you may be pushing thirty, but he'll never see that age again, which suggests an excellent match, in my opinion.'

'In your opinion, General Kirk. Is it as easy as that?' Two pink patches glowed on Molly's cheeks. 'Can't you realize that Bill and I are finished? Have you forgotten who I am? Ryde's niece – a murderer and a sort of parricide, as well. Bill Easter can never marry me. I'm tainted by the blood of that creature down there. Possessed, cursed, by his memory and . . .'

'Shut your mouth and listen to me, Molly Bloom.' Kirk's natural rudeness remained intact. 'Stop thinking that there's any connection between you and Tom Ryde. You may share his genes, but so what? Ryde wasn't a person, but a force. A completely alien being that came into this world by mistake. They occur now and again, like creatures from another galaxy sent to spread mischief on this earth.

'And I killed the first two, didn't I? I'd have put a bullet through Grace as well, if Uncle hadn't stopped me. But does that make me a mass murderer? Not on your Nellie.' The General's whole body shook with righteous conviction, but I tucked the information away for future reference. If Kirk intended to hush up tonight's events, someone else might whisper into a shell-like ear and he'd have some explaining to do. An attractive possibility, but short-lived, and his next remark sent my hopes tumbling.

'Concealing evidence from the police, Billy. That's what you're thinking, so look out of the window and tell me if you see any police about.

'No? How very strange.' I had seen no one, and he grinned horribly. 'Most odd, when this is supposed to be an empty house, and all the lights are on. Surely, at least one rozzer would have come round to investigate?'

I considered the point, which did seem rather ticklish, but Molly answered it. 'Very strange indeed, General, unless they were told to keep away by someone or other.'

'Exactly, my dear, and I was the someone.' Kirk smiled at her. 'The Chief Superintendent fully agreed with me when I telephoned him before we left London. Didn't want any of his brave lads clumping around here in their size thirteen boots. Might have picked up a dose of Tommy's objectionable influence.

'No, Molly. I knew that you were the best bet to stop Tommy Ryde, and you did stop him. Bill and I were almost out cold when you clobbered Grace and cooked the goose perfectly.

'And now, children, I started this affair with a book and that book has to be finished, so either come with me or stay here. The choice is entirely yours.'

So the old fool walked towards the door, and two younger fools followed him. Molly clutched my arm affectionately, but though I was fond of the lass, I didn't care much for her next remark.

'Bad blood, Bill,' she said. 'An unfortunate heredity, but it'll work. I'll see that it works, and you'll pop the question before the middle of the term, when . . .'

'When what?' My heart almost stopped beating. Had the bitch really inherited her uncle's powers, I wondered. Did Mrs Molly Bloom, née Molly Ryde, intend to hypnotize me? If so, she could find another marriage partner, and to hell with her.

'Yes, *when*, darling,' she said, and then deliberately misquoted a line of verse:

> You could not love me, dear, so much,
> Loved you not money more.

'Well, Billy, if you want money, we'll have to make it. When – if – providing that the school production lines can be speeded up, we'll live in modest comfort and you can take half the profits.'

'Fair enough,' I heard myself gasp. Personally, I've never thought that 'gigolo' is an insulting term, and the offer was tempting – extremely tempting and generous – and I paused in the doorway and kissed her with genuine warmth.

Then we headed out after Kirk. Out of Nantmere Lodge, with its ghosts in the basement. Out through the thin, morning sunlight, our bodies pressed together, and I really did love Molly at that moment. Out, towards Kirk's bone-shaking Mercedes, the completion of his book, a sense of duty, a way of life.

His life – not mine. I intended to live the life of Reilly, and though I had no idea who Reilly was, I knew the providers. Molly Bloom and the undisciplined, despicable, industrious toilers at Carthage Road School could look after another Bad Penny.

ALSO AVAILABLE FROM VALANCOURT BOOKS

Michael Arlen	Hell! said the Duchess
R. C. Ashby (Ruby Ferguson)	He Arrived at Dusk
Frank Baker	The Birds
Charles Beaumont	The Hunger and Other Stories
David Benedictus	The Fourth of June
Charles Birkin	The Smell of Evil
John Blackburn	A Scent of New-Mown Hay
	Broken Boy
	Blue Octavo
	The Flame and the Wind
	Nothing but the Night
	Bury Him Darkly
	The Face of the Lion
Thomas Blackburn	The Feast of the Wolf
John Braine	Room at the Top
	The Vodi
R. Chetwynd-Hayes	The Monster Club
Basil Copper	The Great White Space
	Necropolis
Hunter Davies	Body Charge
Jennifer Dawson	The Ha-Ha
Barry England	Figures in a Landscape
Ronald Fraser	Flower Phantoms
Gillian Freeman	The Liberty Man
	The Leather Boys
	The Leader
Stephen Gilbert	Bombardier
	Monkeyface
	The Burnaby Experiments
	Ratman's Notebooks
Martyn Goff	The Youngest Director
Stephen Gregory	The Cormorant
Thomas Hinde	Mr. Nicholas
	The Day the Call Came
Claude Houghton	I Am Jonathan Scrivener
	This Was Ivor Trent
Gerald Kersh	Nightshade and Damnations
	Fowlers End
Francis King	Never Again
	An Air That Kills
	The Dividing Stream
	The Dark Glasses

C.H.B. Kitchin	Ten Pollitt Place
	The Book of Life
Hilda Lewis	The Witch and the Priest
John Lodwick	Brother Death
Kenneth Martin	Aubade
Michael Nelson	Knock or Ring
	A Room in Chelsea Square
Beverley Nichols	Crazy Pavements
Oliver Onions	The Hand of Kornelius Voyt
J.B. Priestley	Benighted
	The Doomsday Men
	The Other Place
	The Magicians
	The Thirty-First of June
	The Shapes of Sleep
	Saturn Over the Water
Peter Prince	Play Things
Piers Paul Read	Monk Dawson
Forrest Reid	Following Darkness
	The Spring Song
	Brian Westby
	The Tom Barber Trilogy
	Denis Bracknel
George Sims	Sleep No More
	The Last Best Friend
Andrew Sinclair	The Facts in the Case of E.A. Poe
	The Raker
Colin Spencer	Panic
David Storey	Radcliffe
	Pasmore
	Saville
Russell Thorndike	The Slype
	The Master of the Macabre
John Wain	Hurry on Down
	The Smaller Sky
	Strike the Father Dead
	A Winter in the Hills
Keith Waterhouse	There is a Happy Land
	Billy Liar
Colin Wilson	Ritual in the Dark
	Man Without a Shadow
	The World of Violence
	The Philosopher's Stone
	The God of the Labyrinth